The Lieutenant Takes the Sky

SELECTED FICTION WORKS BY
L. RON HUBBARD

FANTASY
The Case of the Friendly Corpse

Death's Deputy

Fear

The Ghoul

The Indigestible Triton

Slaves of Sleep & The Masters of Sleep

Typewriter in the Sky

The Ultimate Adventure

SCIENCE FICTION
Battlefield Earth

The Conquest of Space

The End Is Not Yet

Final Blackout

The Kilkenny Cats

The Kingslayer

The Mission Earth Dekalogy*

Ole Doc Methuselah

To the Stars

ADVENTURE
The Hell Job series

WESTERN
Buckskin Brigades

Empty Saddles

Guns of Mark Jardine

Hot Lead Payoff

A full list of L. Ron Hubbard's
novellas and short stories is provided at the back.

*Dekalogy—a group of ten volumes

L. RON HUBBARD

The Lieutenant Takes the Sky

Published by
Galaxy Press, LLC
7051 Hollywood Boulevard, Suite 200
Hollywood, CA 90028

Printed in the United States of America.

ISBN-10 1-59212-322-8
ISBN-13 978-1-59212-322-3

Library of Congress Control Number: 2007903613

Contents

Stories from Pulp Fiction's Golden Age

A ND it *was* a golden age. The 1930s and 1940s were a vibrant, seminal time for a gigantic audience of eager readers, probably the largest per capita audience of readers in American history. The magazine racks were chock-full of publications with ragged trims, garish cover art, cheap brown pulp paper, low cover prices—and the most excitement you could hold in your hands.

"Pulp" magazines, named for their rough-cut, pulpwood paper, were a vehicle for more amazing tales than Scheherazade could have told in a million and one nights. Set apart from higher-class "slick" magazines, printed on fancy glossy paper with quality artwork and superior production values, the pulps were for the "rest of us," adventure story after adventure story for people who liked to *read*. Pulp fiction authors were no-holds-barred entertainers—real storytellers. They were more interested in a thrilling plot twist, a horrific villain or a white-knuckle adventure than they were in lavish prose or convoluted metaphors.

The sheer volume of tales released during this wondrous golden age remains unmatched in any other period of literary history—hundreds of thousands of published stories in over nine hundred different magazines. Some titles lasted only an issue or two; many magazines succumbed to paper shortages during World War II, while others endured for decades yet. Pulp fiction remains as a treasure trove of stories you can read, stories you can love, stories you can remember. The stories were driven by plot and character, with grand heroes, terrible villains, beautiful damsels (often in distress), diabolical plots, amazing places, breathless romances. The readers wanted to be taken beyond the mundane, to live adventures far removed from their ordinary lives—and the pulps rarely failed to deliver.

In that regard, pulp fiction stands in the tradition of all memorable literature. For as history has shown, good stories are much more than fancy prose. William Shakespeare, Charles Dickens, Jules Verne, Alexandre Dumas—many of the greatest literary figures wrote their fiction for the readers, not simply literary colleagues and academic admirers. And writers for pulp magazines were no exception. These publications reached an audience that dwarfed the circulations of today's short story magazines. Issues of the pulps were scooped up and read by over thirty million avid readers each month.

Because pulp fiction writers were often paid no more than a cent a word, they had to become prolific or starve. They also had to write aggressively. As Richard Kyle, publisher and editor of *Argosy*, the first and most long-lived of the pulps, so pointedly explained: "The pulp magazine writers, the best of them, worked for markets that did not write for critics or attempt to satisfy timid advertisers. Not having to answer to anyone other than their readers, they wrote about human beings on the edges of the unknown, in those new lands the future would explore. They wrote for what we would become, not for what we had already been."

Some of the more lasting names that graced the pulps include H. P. Lovecraft, Edgar Rice Burroughs, Robert E. Howard, Max Brand, Louis L'Amour, Elmore Leonard, Dashiell Hammett, Raymond Chandler, Erle Stanley Gardner, John D. MacDonald, Ray Bradbury, Isaac Asimov, Robert Heinlein—and, of course, L. Ron Hubbard.

In a word, he was among the most prolific and popular writers of the era. He was also the most enduring—hence this series—and certainly among the most legendary. It all began only months after he first tried his hand at fiction, with L. Ron Hubbard tales appearing in *Thrilling Adventures, Argosy, Five-Novels Monthly, Detective Fiction Weekly, Top-Notch, Texas Ranger, War Birds, Western Stories,* even *Romantic Range.* He could write on any subject, in any genre, from jungle explorers to deep-sea divers, from G-men and gangsters, cowboys and flying aces to mountain climbers, hard-boiled detectives and spies. But he really began to shine when he turned his talent to science fiction and fantasy of which he authored nearly fifty novels or novelettes to forever change the shape of those genres.

Following in the tradition of such famed authors as Herman Melville, Mark Twain, Jack London and Ernest Hemingway, Ron Hubbard actually lived adventures that his own characters would have admired—as an ethnologist among primitive tribes, as prospector and engineer in hostile climes, as a captain of vessels on four oceans. He even wrote a series of articles for *Argosy*, called "Hell Job," in which he lived and told of the most dangerous professions a man could put his hand to.

Finally, and just for good measure, he was also an accomplished photographer, artist, filmmaker, musician and educator. But he was first and foremost a *writer*, and that's the L. Ron Hubbard we come to know through the pages of this volume.

This library of Stories from the Golden Age presents the best of L. Ron Hubbard's fiction from the heyday of storytelling, the Golden Age of the pulp magazines. In these eighty volumes, readers are treated to a full banquet of 153 stories, a kaleidoscope of tales representing every imaginable genre: science fiction, fantasy, western, mystery, thriller, horror, even romance—action of all kinds and in all places.

Because the pulps themselves were printed on such inexpensive paper with high acid content, issues were not meant to endure. As the years go by, the original issues of every pulp from *Argosy* through *Zeppelin Stories* continue crumbling into brittle, brown dust. This library preserves the L. Ron Hubbard tales from that era, presented with a distinctive look that brings back the nostalgic flavor of those times.

L. Ron Hubbard's Stories from the Golden Age has something for every taste, every reader. These tales will return you to a time when fiction was good clean entertainment and the most fun a kid could have on a rainy afternoon or the best thing an adult could enjoy after a long day at work.

Pick up a volume, and remember what reading is supposed to be all about. Remember curling up with a *great story*.

—Kevin J. Anderson

KEVIN J. ANDERSON *is the author of more than ninety critically acclaimed works of speculative fiction, including* The Saga of Seven Suns, *the continuation of the Dune Chronicles with Brian Herbert, and his* New York Times *bestselling novelization of L. Ron Hubbard's* Ai! Pedrito!

The Lieutenant
Takes the Sky

Chapter One

I T was dark in the prison; too dark to see the rats that fought for breadcrumbs before the door. Aiming by sound alone, Mike Malloy threw a savage shoe. There was a squeak of protest and the hurried patter of the retreat.

"Why the hell did I do that?" said Mike to himself. "I can't eat the stuff."

He groped for his shoe across the pave worn smooth by centuries of polishing by the restless condemned. At last he sat back in the corner, the straw damp beneath him, and put his shoe on again.

The rats came forth anew, but with more caution. Soon, reassured, they were battling over the crumbs again.

"You guys are lucky," said Mike Malloy. "If there was some way I could reincarnate in reverse to a rat and go out under that door . . ." He sighed deeply and was silent. But the place was too still, and he hid his creeps by speaking anew. "Rats, I'll give you some advice. Never sock a colonel, no matter how badly he needs it. And for that matter, rats, never sock a lieutenant colonel. And I might add that it is also unlucky to swab a deck with a general's aide. It gets his clothes dirty and he doesn't like it."

With this caution he subsided.

"Rats, I'll give you some advice. Never sock a colonel, no matter how badly he needs it."

A sound came throbbing into the cell; a plane droned high in the Moroccan blue. It brought melancholy to Mike Malloy. It was the sound of freedom, the sound of excitement and clean sun on flashing wings.

"If I had it to do all over again," he sighed, "I . . . hell, there's no use to lie about it. I'd sock the colonel and the lieutenant colonel and his aide just the same."

The rats grew quiet at the sound of his voice and then fell to on the banquet once more.

"Let that be a lesson to you," said Mike. "Don't lie, always be honest and upright, thank God for your blessings, and check your engine before you take off. Never argue with your superiors and be a good soldier in all things, and someday," he said impressively, "someday you'll be where I am. That, my furry friends, is the secret of success. Once I was a private . . ."

Boot beats sounded in the corridor and Mike, though he had no hope, sat alertly listening. Arms grounded with a rhythmic thud and a key grated.

A corporal, looking satanic, lifted his lantern to the height of his head and studied the cell, trying to locate Mike.

Mike got up. He bowed courteously. "Gentlemen, you honor me. Come in by all means, and have some crumbs with the rest of the rats."

"*Sacré nom d'un cochon . . .*" sputtered the corporal.

"I didn't call you pigs," said Mike. "I said 'rats.' Come, my good fellow. The general has, of course, sent for me to extend his apologies."

The corporal blinked rapidly. "*M'sieu le capitaine,* you astound me! How is it that you knew?"

Mike found that it was his turn to blink, and he did so. "You mean . . . ?" he gaped.

"Why, but yes. The general is very urgently requesting your presence immediately. But I cannot understand how you . . ."

"Huh," said Mike, "there's a catch to this someplace. Last time I heard from the army, I was outward bound to a penal battalion. How come the sudden change of heart?"

"*M'sieu le capitaine,* I am but a corporal of the armies of France. The policy of generals—"

"What?" said Mike. "They don't consult you? But come, my favorite rodent, lead me forward—though I'm not sure but what it would be smarter to stay where I am."

He stepped into the files and the corporal barked commands and they moved off.

Mike Malloy

Chapter Two

CAPTAIN Mike Malloy was conducted to the general's office with great speed. Before the door, the files grounded their Lebels with a loud crash and the corporal threw the portal wide.

The people in the office turned. General LeRoi gave a start and scowled.

He had not expected his order to be so promptly carried out, and he had never imagined for an instant that Captain Mike Malloy of the French Air Service could be anything but neat. Just now, Mike was not at all polished. A week in jail had taken away all gloss. His beard was dark; his tunic was ripped from shoulder to waist, and the flapping cloth almost obscured his pilot's wings; the bill of his dusty kepi was broken and, all in all, his condition yelled, "Dungeons!"

But for all that Mike was cool enough. He pushed his kepi to the back of his head and walked out of the guard file and into the office. He stopped before the general's desk, looking neither right nor left.

"You sent for me, sir?"

"I did!" said LeRoi, white mustaches bristling and ruddy face scarlet. "You seem to be somewhat untidy."

"No illusion about it," said Mike. "Your observation is correct."

Delage

LeRoi coughed and glared, and then gradually composed himself through necessity.

"Captain Malloy, I wish to introduce you to *M'm'selle* Lois DuGanne," said the general.

Mike turned and then blushed for the wretchedness of his appearance. Lois DuGanne, a little bewildered, nodded to him and gave him a slight smile. Mike bowed but he did not lower his glance. She was a very lovely woman, all neat and crisp in delicate whites. Her eyes were blue and frank. Mike was spellbound.

The general coughed to distract Mike's attention.

"And," said LeRoi loudly, "I wish to present you to *M.* Delage, and his secretary, Henri Corvault."

Mike turned to shake Delage's hand. The man was patently important. His linen was expensive, and was cut on the pattern of most French politicians'. He was around forty, and there was a certain arresting quality about him which one could trace to his eyes. They were odd, those eyes, because it was impossible to tell their exact color.

Henri, the secretary, was too thin to throw a decent shadow. His head was too big for his body and his neck too small. He seemed to be a very timid echo of Delage.

"Captain Malloy," said General LeRoi, "is the man I have

been telling you about. He has just returned from scout duty and I apologize for his appearance. However, it has nothing to do with his competence. He knows every square inch of the Middle Atlas, having fought throughout the last campaign in that region, and he is one of our best pilots."

Mike looked on in amazement and heard in astonishment such praise.

"In addition, we will send with you our Lieutenant Reynard, who is also an excellent pilot," continued LeRoi. "I doubt you will suffer any inconveniences on your trip."

Delage stood up. "General, I am very pleased at your generosity. I could have hoped for nothing more satisfactory."

"*M.* Delage," said the general, "it is with extreme pleasure that I am able to extend to you the courtesies of the French Army. It is little enough to do for such an important personage as yourself."

They bowed to each other.

Miss DuGanne stood up. "And I too thank you, General."

"*M'm'selle,*" said LeRoi, "while I regret your insistence upon accompanying the party into the Middle Atlas—which I assure you is no place for a lovely woman—I shall nevertheless do all in my power to aid you."

Reynard

Henri scuttled to the door and opened it for Delage. The personage bowed in the entrance to the general and then to Mike. "We shall see you in the morning, Captain."

Miss DuGanne smiled at the two officers and withdrew.

When the door had closed, Mike looked with suspicion at LeRoi. "If you don't mind my saying so, sir, it's hardly the time for an expedition of a private sort—"

"Nobody asked your opinion," snapped LeRoi, sitting down. "Why did they have to bring you here in that condition! If you could see yourself . . . !"

"Sir, I assure you that if I had had time, and if I had known, I would have presented another facet of my glittering self. But your guards are most abrupt and your jail . . . General, you should look into that jail."

"None of your insolence, Malloy. You were brought here for one purpose and one purpose only. You can go to the *bataillon pénal,* as scheduled, or you can fly this party into the Middle Atlas. I give you that choice."

Mike was suspicious. "By any chance, would the Middle Atlas trip be worse than the *bataillon pénal*?"

"Probably," snapped LeRoi. "You know the conditions inland as well as I do. Berbers sniping at planes, strange troop movements, and the lid about to blow off all Morocco. I chose you because I would not order an officer on such duty—"

"You are ordering Lieutenant Reynard," said Mike.

"Yes, Lieutenant Reynard. He has committed one too many murders in the name of espionage. As he cannot be censured for doing his duty, I can only send him on such a mission."

Mike was very puzzled by now. "Sir, if it is going to be as bad as all that, how can you send such an important man as *M.* Delage into the interior—"

"I send him nowhere," corrected LeRoi. "*M.* Delage is much less important than he himself thinks. He is a small-time politician in France, has some remote connection with the French Academy and, through ignorance, has selected this time to go searching for a book in the Middle Atlas."

"A book?" said Mike.

"Yes. I understand that it is the girl's idea. She is an American and, like you, seems to be crazy. The book is *L'Aud,* the only volume missing from the Karaouine University Library. It has been gone for eight hundred years, and was last in the possession of Sultan Ibn Tumart. I believe it contained an alchemical formula for the manufacture of gold from base metals. That is all pure bosh, but these three people are crazy to go on their trip, and they have asked the French Army to help them. Very well, help them we shall. But they will also help us."

"I don't understand," said Mike.

"You wouldn't," snapped LeRoi. "If I were to send a squadron of scouting planes into the Middle Atlas, all hell would break loose. You know it and I know it. We cannot afford to start Allal Fassei's uprising for him by making the first move."

Mike knew about that. The mysterious organizer of the very apparent disaffection of Morocco's populace, Allal Fassei, was as elusive as a gale of wind. He was felt, but never seen. It was thought that he was some fanatical Berber out preaching the jihad, but one could never be too sure. Here today and gone tomorrow, and never once had either army espionage or soldiery set eyes upon him.

"Allal Fassei," said the general, "must be located. His movements in the Middle Atlas must be uncovered. Now, attend. The last of five agents sent into the Middle Atlas has failed to report after two weeks. Lieutenant Fereaux has evidently been discovered by the Berbers, and you know the things the Berbers do. Very well, we cannot afford to waste more agents or more time ferreting out the intentions of Allal Fassei. We must find out if there is any troop concentration in the Atlas of any kind, and be prepared to meet it. You and Reynard will have the cover of this expedition. It is doubtful if you will be suspected immediately. You are to get that information and bring it to us as fast as you can."

"Sounds like sudden death to me," said Mike.

"Men do not leave the *bataillon pénal* after a year—and your sentence is five."

"Oh, I'm not kicking," said Mike, "but it seems a shame to use civilians as pawns—"

"You're thinking of that girl. Malloy, you are to give no consideration to the fate of these people. Compared to the safety of every white man in Morocco, their lives are nothing. This is the way wars are fought, and this is the way a soldier must carry on. Feelings have nothing to do with duty."

"Yes, yes, yes," sighed Mike. "But just the same, that girl is much too—"

"Your attention will be for Allal Fassei. All of your attention, mind. His movements must be spotted and, if possible, his identity uncovered."

"And if we all get killed?" said Mike.

"That would be most unsoldierly of you," said LeRoi, "and very ungrateful. However, know that if you are killed, your family would probably forget many things about you and remember you as a hero."

"That is most solacing," said Mike.

"Report to the drome in the morning," said LeRoi. "If you don't I'll have you shot as a deserter. Good day, Captain."

"Good day," said Mike, walking slowly out.

Chapter Three

IN the chill desert morning, with the world still half-asleep, Captain Mike Malloy examined the two observation ships which had been allotted to *M*. Delage and party. They had been posted the night before, and so it was with some surprise that he could find nothing wrong with the planes. He had at least thought to discover a time bomb in a cockpit. Morocco, of late, had been like that.

He was just completing his search when he heard a slight rustling sound on the other side of the fuselage. He knew better than to straighten up. Abruptly he jackknifed.

A knife shrieked through fabric where he had stood an instant before.

On his knees, Mike saw a pair of bare feet under the ship. He snatched at the ankles and yanked back.

With a yelp of terror, the would-be assassin laid hold of the tail skid and refused to be pried away from it. He was evidently a Karaouine student, from the cut of his djellaba and his fanatical intention, as well as the well-bred way he swore.

"Let go!" ordered Mike, pulling hard.

A very smooth voice behind Malloy said, "Ah, we have trouble already."

Still holding the ankles, Mike turned to see Lieutenant

Reynard. That exquisitely handsome officer had once been known as *M'sieu Toutou* of the Paris underworld—before France needed him in its espionage corps.

With the hard toe of his boot, Reynard kicked the assassin's fingers away from the tail skid. He bent over and clutched at the dark throat, and his metallic eyes drilled holes through the man's skull.

"Who sent you?" said Reynard. "Quick, talk! Who sent you? Tell and you can go. Refuse to tell and you greet *Shaitan*."

The Karaouine man, a Hadith in the making, returned the glare. "Foreign swine! Kill me or not, but you have but little time to live yourself!"

"Then you say no?" queried Reynard.

"Wait," said Malloy. "He—"

"Tried to stab you in the back," said Reynard.

There was a muffled explosion. Mike had not even seen Reynard draw. The smoke lifted greasily away from the side of the embryo-Hadith's head.

In disgust Mike dropped the twitching ankles. "You didn't have to do that, Reynard."

"Bah, they're better off dead. You are too soft. You have too much heart! You take the part of a flogged black man and batter down staff officers, and almost go to the penal battalion. And now, *ma foi*, you plead for the life of a man who just tried to kill you. *Capitaine*, an Irishman is bad enough. But an Irishman who is also an American . . . *Dieu!*"

"Oh!" said a startled voice, beyond the wing.

Mike hurriedly tried to shove the corpse out of sight. But

she had already seen it. Lois DuGanne's face was the color of paper.

"*Mam'selle,*" said Reynard with a sweeping bow, "we regret subjecting you to the sight of a corpse, but—"

Mike kicked Reynard in the ankle. "My apologies, Miss DuGanne."

Fascinated with horror, she could not look away. Suddenly Mike understood that this girl was lately out of glittering salons and was probably looking at her first dead man. He stepped around the wing and took her arm.

"You go in this other plane," said Mike, trying to lead her away.

She recovered herself and angrily jerked away from him. "Please, Captain, keep your hands to yourself." She stared at those hands as though she could see blood on them.

Mike shrugged. "Anyway, that's still your plane over there."

She was very cool. "May I ask which one you intend to pilot?"

"That one over there—in which you are going to ride."

"Thank you so much," said Lois DuGanne, "but I prefer the other—if you don't mind." She turned and started to walk, but she stopped.

Reynard had not seen her before. He had reason to believe that he was a devil with the ladies—did Reynard. And he was greatly intrigued by Lois DuGanne's wavy brown hair and lovely face, and the way the morning breeze pressed the white sport suit against her.

Uncertainly she looked at Reynard. His mouth curved down into a grin and his eyes ate her up.

Lois faced about and walked rapidly toward Mike's ship. Mike grinned after her. "Thanks, Reynard."

"What?" said Reynard.

Delage and Henri had arrived, burdened with boxes and grips. Henri was completely obliterated by baggage.

"Ah, good morning, Captain," said Delage. "I would say that your appearance has greatly improved. Clean khaki and a shave practically make a gentleman out of you."

"Practically," said Mike. "Where do you think you're going to store those boxes?"

"Why, in the plane. I say," said Delage, "you've two observation planes here. Isn't there a cabin ship available? After all, desert wind and sun—"

"We're taking two ships that can fight," said Mike.

"Fight?" blinked Henri with a gulp.

"If you think I'm going to tour the Middle Atlas in an ice-wagon," said Mike, "you're crazy. Allal Fassei has several squadrons scattered through Morocco."

"Allal Fassei?" said Delage. "I have heard that name before. Isn't he in the pay of the totalitarian powers, to restore Morocco to—"

"To give Morocco to the dictators," said Mike. "He's the shadow over the land, according to the Arabs. Nobody knows who he is or where he is but we've felt his weight now and then. For instance . . ." Mutely he pointed to the body under the fuselage.

"Ugh!" said Henri. "He's . . . he's dead!"

"Of a certainty, gentlemen," said Reynard. "A bullet placed just *so* and a trigger squeezed just *so* . . ."

"Captain," said Delage, "do you expect trouble?"

"Trouble tags me around like a hound dog," said Mike. "Find Mrs. Malloy's little boy Mike, and you find trouble right beside him. But we haven't any time to stand here talking. You can't take all that baggage. Put it down and I'll have a mechanic take care of it for you. We've got to get out of here before the air gets rough. You'll be sick enough, I'll bet, when we get over the Atlas. Jacques! Take this baggage to the hangar and store it. *M'sieu* Delage, you and Henri Corvault will please ride with Lieutenant Reynard. My ship over there has a sun hood, and Miss DuGanne's complexion, I am sure, would suffer more than yours."

Henri looked as though he was about to object. But Delage shrugged, and so Henri shrugged. The mechanic took the boxes away, and a squad bore off the body of the Hadith-never-to-be.

Mike climbed into his ship and stood up in the slipstream, surveying the field and air before them as he buckled on his helmet. He settled down into the pit and buckled his belt. Sliding the tinted glass hood over the cockpits with his right hand, he smiled at Miss DuGanne. "Keeps you from getting burned. Buckle your belt and . . . say, get into your chute!"

"Why?"

Mike looked at her with wonder. "Haven't you heard that planes sometimes go to pieces in the air?"

"They don't just go to pieces," said Miss DuGanne.

"When bullets hit them they do."

"Bullets?" she gasped.

"Say, look here," said Mike. "Did you think this was going to be a Sunday school picnic?"

"Why, no, but—"

"Allal Fassei is likely to strike any day now, and if he does and we happen to be in the Middle Atlas, we're in for some fun. If you'll pardon my saying so, this is a hell of a time to go off looking for a book on alchemy. If you weren't wise to the political situation, maybe you'd like to cancel the engagement. You . . . well . . . you're too pretty to get full of lead."

"You doubt my courage?"

"Not after that question," said Mike, "but I sure have got a low opinion of your common sense."

He waved for the chocks to be pulled and cracked his palm against the throttle, and the swift craft streaked out across the golden sand, to lighten and then spring into the air.

Behind them came Reynard.

Far ahead, like pink clouds along the horizon, loomed the Atlas.

Chapter Four

L OIS DUGANNE watched the captain's back. Now that she did not have to talk to him, she could try to form some estimation of him. And two facts were at war within her. Captain Mike Malloy, crisp in fresh khaki, was a very handsome fellow, black-eyed, gay and dashing. And he was undoubtedly a calloused scoundrel who could kill a man without a second thought, whose lot was prison, and who did not have a very savory reputation in the army. All the evidence she had was slim but, at the same time, she had seen it with her own eyes.

The problem of his presence baffled her. She had hardly expected an American in the uniform of a French flight captain. He was not of the *Legions Étrangères*. She knew about that. He was regular army.

Quite definitely she knew she could not trust him. Too fresh in mind was the terrifying picture he had presented to her the day before—his hair sticking out from under his cap, his tunic torn and his face a mass of dirty beard. She was certain that no respectable officer would ever allow himself to descend to such a depth.

And while she mused, she was conscious of a small sound which recurred three times to be followed by a fluttering, rapid staccato. She looked around and saw that a strip of fabric had become unloosened on the right wing and was now cracking in the breeze. And more, she saw, the instant she looked, a hole appear farther out. It was a very little hole, and the resultant sound was small. But another strip of fabric peeled back from it.

She looked down and beheld men, doll-like from this height, jumping up and down and shaking their fists and rifles at the plane whose shadow sailed unconcernedly over them.

"They're shooting at us!" she cried in Mike's ear.

He was startled by the loudness and closeness of her voice. "You didn't think they'd throw us kisses, did you? Or did you?"

"You're not nice," said Lois.

"Neither are they," said Mike. "If we weren't going places, I'd go back and let some of the high blood pressure out of them."

"But why should they shoot at us?"

"Lady," said Mike, "you are riding in a plane with a French tricolor on it."

"I know that, but why—?"

"Are you dumb?" said Mike, facing around, "or don't you know anything at all about Morocco?"

"Why, yes . . . I mean no. I always had a picture of this land as one of date palms and camels and Bedouins and sunlight. . . ."

"Well, forget it," said Mike. "This is the land of body lice and . . . Aw, what's the use. You'll know soon enough. The French are supporting Sidi Mohammed, the sultan in power, and they don't worry about little things like anti-government propaganda. They're too lenient on the boys, and an Arab or a Riff or a Berber can't understand that. So the populace is listening to the sweet song of Allal Fassei. Boy, if this government ever is overturned, the brown lads will find out how easy they had it before. And the point of all this is, we're bound for the Middle Atlas where the Berbers never have been really whipped. And so, Allal Fassei's song of 'freedom' is finding fertile ground. From the place we're going will come the shock troops of the uprising—when and if it occurs."

"But why don't they arrest this Allal Fassei?" said Lois.

"Why . . . Look, instead of scratching, why doesn't a dog find the flea and kill it?"

"Maybe he can't."

"Right," said Mike Malloy. He turned to her again. "Look, I feel kind of responsible for you. Are you sure you couldn't let this business wait a few months? Say the word and I'll turn back. . . ."

"Captain Malloy, my uncle dreamed for thirty years of finding *L'Aud*. He never could, because of bad health and lack of money. He's dead now, but I'd like to . . . well fulfill his dream for him. And there's something else. He expended so much money in the search that . . . well, there's none left. A year and a half ago I communicated with the French Society of Archaeology, stating that I had some evidence supporting a probable location of *L'Aud* which vanished about eight hundred years ago. They wrote that *M.* Delage had expressed an interest. But it was not until last month that *M.* Delage cabled me that he was willing to help me and would accompany me and finance the search. I took what funds I had and—"

"And you can't turn back now, even if you wanted to," said Mike.

"Yes. I guess that's it."

"But, hell, a lovely woman like you doesn't belong out here in *le Maroc!* You . . . you belong in a salon with—"

"That's where I was. A salon in New York City. Modeling clothes for the Four Hundred. If you've ever stood on your feet eight hours a day, holding up your arms and having women paw at you . . ."

"They never do," said Mike with a sigh.

He banked sharply, and she looked down to see a rifleman dismounted and pointing his gun skyward. Even as she looked, a puff of white smoke rolled from the muzzle. She could not tell whether the bullet hit the plane or not.

"Don't worry," said Mike. "They're damned good shots, but when rifles bring down fast planes, we'll stop flying. . . . So you were a model, after your uncle sunk the wherewithal into a crazy stunt to recover an alchemical formula. Say, just who is this guy Delage?"

"He's very important," said Lois.

"Obviously," ambiguously replied Mike.

"Politically," said Lois.

"He ought to know better than to drag you across *le Maroc* at such a time. Of course it did me a favor."

"How so? I gained the impression that you disliked this duty."

"If I hadn't taken it, I would now be marching off to the penal battalion," said Mike, "and so I am duly grateful."

"But . . . but what did you do?"

"Oh, nothing much. Beat up a colonel and a lieutenant colonel and an aide. I fear that the aide was the mistake. He had a glass jaw."

"Must you fight?"

"Must Irishmen be born?" said Mike.

"You are Irish, aren't you—without any dilution."

"You're wrong there. I've got some French in me too. Ever hear of the Irish Guard?"

"Why, yes! They were formed in Napoleon's time. They were his bodyguard."

"To the head of the class," said Mike. "And ever since that time the French get weak minded once in a while and put an Irishman through the Sorbonne, which technically makes a Frenchman out of him."

"But I thought one had to be a gentleman—" She stopped. "I'm sorry."

"No need to be sorry," said Mike. "You behold Michael Ste. Marie Jacques Malloi Du Vincennes in the flesh. Lately returned from Spain, more lately from Cochin China, and at present flying a lovely young lady over *le Maroc*."

"Du Vincennes!" said Lois, impressed. "Why . . . why, I remember my uncle talking for days because a Du Vincennes had spoken to him in Paris. How is it that . . ."

"*Mam'selle*, you behold the dark-hued lamb of the tribe. If I even start for Paris, there's a riot."

"But why?"

25

"Why not?" said Mike. "My father was the same way. He deserted with the colonel's wife and fled to New York. And the family forgave the son and then the son . . . but why go on?"

"You mean you're in disgrace?"

"Dear lady, what a weak word. There is a standing order on the army lists that I be thrown to the wolves the instant there's the slightest excuse. Witness my arrest. All I did . . ."

"I know, but surely, there must have been some reason in the first place."

"Oh, yes," said Mike, cheerfully. "I lost a hundred thousand francs at Monte Carlo and carelessly signed my grandfather's name. I explained that it was to save the family honor but it was no use. They said it was forgery. And then I killed a lieutenant in Saigon. . . ."

"Forgery? Murder?"

"It wasn't murder. It was a duel. However his father was Minister of War. And then there was the case of a girl at the Follies Ber—"

"Please don't go on," said Lois weakly.

"But I only tried to protect my cousin. I was already in bad so I thought it would be a shame . . ."

"Please," begged Lois.

"Well, then," said Mike, "I was squadron treasurer and the funds vanished and they said embezzlement . . ."

"Of course all these things just happened," said Lois.

"That's right," said Mike. "Everywhere I go there's trouble. So the family threw me over at last . . ."

"I should think they would!"

"And if I get out of this alive, I'll . . ."

"You really believe that this is dangerous?"

"Lady," said Mike, banking again to throw off the combined aim of a village below, "this is no picnic." He pointed up through the hood. "See?"

It took her some time to see what he meant, because her eyes were not accustomed to the limitless reaches of the azure heavens.

Less than the cross of a pencil five thousand feet above them, hovered a plane. It was neither diving nor was it running away. It was matching their speed mile for mile.

Finally she turned and looked back to see that Reynard was at their own height about a thousand yards behind them. Again she looked at the strange plane.

"But who could that be?" she said. "I can make out no insignia."

"The eyes of Allal Fassei," replied Mike. "Buckle your chute over your shoulders."

With a sinking sensation she stared earthward. They had begun to cross the first barren reaches of the craggy Atlas. All below was tumbled dun rocks and miserable scrubs of trees. Not for miles was there a landing place.

"Once," said Mike, "those gentlemen rode battle barbs and flourished lances and sang poetry. Now they squat behind machine guns and carry grenades and fly, and swear in gutter French. Civilization, dear lady, is a great boon to the world."

He had clicked on his radiophone and his fingers rolled the dials. He pressed his helmet phones closer to his head, listening. Then he shrugged. "It's all in code, but I can guess what he's saying. Sorry, but hold on tight. We're going up."

"You mean . . ."

Full out, the engine began to grind on the climb, its hoarse song a challenge to battle.

It was impossible for the girl to keep the other ship in sight. The French observation plane could climb so swiftly that the earth fell with violence away from them.

And then, above the engine's roar, she heard a chattering burst of sound. A round hole appeared in the glass hood, and slivers of glass rained upon her.

Then she saw the other ship. It had been diving to meet them, and now, at terrific speed, it was flashing level and firing as it came. The air about the French plane was lined like a spider web with straight lines of tracer.

She did not know the disadvantage under which Mike fought. In a ship designed for a rear cockpit machine gunner, he had to fight with bow guns only. But he fought.

The bottom fell out of the sky. Terrified, the girl looked up and saw the earth. She was hurled back into her seat, and her head felt as if it would split apart under the concussions of the rattling guns. Her nostrils were seared with cordite smoke, and a hot empty flipped back to burn her hand.

Again she saw the other ship. It had looped away and now was coming back. She saw a pair of flashing goggles, a head cloth fluttering in the wind. . . .

Suddenly she knew that there were two ships attacking them, not one. And Reynard was still far below, struggling up to the fight, but retarded by his extra passenger.

Earth and sky were a jumble of peaks and clouds, spinning like a maelstrom. Again Mike's machine guns yammered.

Ahead, straight ahead, the first plane strove to scuttle out of range. Above, the other was streaking for home.

Flame streaked back into the other's slipstream. With a growing yowl which was loud above the French engine, the plane began a swooping, sickening series of dives, painting the skies black with oil smoke.

Finally the pilot got free. He bailed out, a small ball falling through the blue, toward the jagged earth below. A banner streamed from him and then, with a jerk, the chute filled.

Lois felt sick, but she could not take her eyes from the scene below.

Reynard had climbed a short ways. Reynard dived, and long black lines lanced from the French ship's nose toward the helplessly spinning pilot who swung from silk in the blue.

Twice, thrice the black lines raked.

Again Reynard fired. The silk ignited from the tracer, and great gouts of colorless flame flashed as the chute was devoured.

The small ball was again tumbling through space. And then it was a dot upon the rough earth.

*With a growing yowl which was loud above the French engine,
the plane began a swooping, sickening series of dives,
painting the skies black with oil smoke.*

Chapter Five

THE coolness of sunset came to the small field high in the Middle Atlas where night winds were chill. Staked to earth, the two planes crouched like fabulous beasts about to spring.

The small tents had been erected, and now Reynard and Mike were setting a Lewis gun into an emplacement, as a precaution against attack.

"It was excellent teamwork, eh?" said Reynard, mentioning the air fight for the first time.

"Don't include me in that teamwork," said Mike.

"But you —"

"Yes, I shot him down. He was a slower ship and I shot him out of the air. But get this, Reynard—I do not kill men in parachutes."

"Ah, you are squeamish because of that woman, no? You know and I know that next time we meet that ship it would have ten with it, and *we* would be dead men. You and I know that these fellows have a hard time getting pilots, a hard time getting planes. Well, *voilà*. One plane and one pilot less. You know the orders issued these many months ago to all of us. Make no reports on planes met and downed and pilots killed, unless they are our own. She is not war, Mike, she is not revolt. She is nice, legal murder."

31

"Shut up," said Mike. "Here comes Miss DuGanne."

Reynard looked at Mike and then unwillingly walked away. Mike busied himself with loading the machine gun.

"Are there no people in these mountains?" said Lois.

"People? Certainly. Some sniper may have his sights lined up on you this very minute," said Mike brutally.

She glanced at the heights about them. "I can't bring myself to believe that the government would allow us to walk into such danger. And Captain, that unnecessary shooting this afternoon—"

"Unnecessary shooting is not a very neat way of putting it," said Mike. "He would have spotted our landing place if I hadn't done for him. As it is, there's a chance that we will not be immediately found. There are several such fields which we use. We might have gone to any one of them—"

"But to kill him when he was helpless!"

"Dear lady, this happens to be *le Maroc*. Harems and date palms and camels are all right in the geographies, but they don't go far enough. Harem women are mostly enslaved against their will, dates are horrible as a steady diet and camels bite. And it happens that a few dead men more or less are the least of *l'Africain's* concern. And as for the government worrying unduly about you . . ." He shrugged and tested the firing pin before he put a shell under it. The rays of the dying sun flashed on his ring.

She looked at it wonderingly. Mike Malloy did not seem the kind of man who would wear a ring of that description. Uneasily she sensed importance in that scowling, bright-eyed face of gold.

32

"That is a pretty ring," she said.

"This? Oh, yes. My great-uncle Oscar gave it to me with his dying breath. It's a bad-luck charm."

"What?"

"Well, everybody wears good-luck charms. I am different. I wear bad-luck charms."

A rumbling chuckle sounded nearby and Mike spun about to see Delage and Henri. Delage looked at the ring.

"Egyptian," he announced. "Rather neat piece of work. Would you like to sell it, Captain?"

"Sell it? Oh, I don't think so. It is but a bauble."

"But extremely interesting," said Delage. "There is one like it in the Louvre. But . . . why, these don't look like real diamonds."

"Probably glass," said Mike. "My great-uncle Oscar was false to the end, I suppose."

"Ah, well," smiled Delage, "it's pretty, anyway. I suppose we'll start combing the country about here tomorrow. I am very keen on finding the tomb and returning. That incident this afternoon was not so very pleasant. I had no idea that powder smoke was so acrid. Perhaps there is some small truth in the rumors concerning the restlessness of Morocco these days."

"Perhaps," said Mike. "Where there is—"

"Hullo!" cried Reynard, from across the field. "Come over here!"

They went toward him swiftly. Mike was in the lead, and he caught a glimpse of what Reynard had found. "Please, Miss DuGanne. Keep back."

He walked slowly forward. Reynard was standing beside a thing which had once been a man. The arms and legs had been staked out so that the poor devil had had to face the sun. The lids of his eyes had been cut away. Twigs had been thrust through his cheeks.

Pointing to some crude knife work, Reynard said, "The women finished him up."

Something glittered on the dried hand and caught Delage's attention. He knelt down. "Why . . . why, it's a ring just like yours!" he said to Mike. He looked at Reynard. "And you have one, too! But why should they leave such a bit of jewelry as this ring?"

"Get a shovel, Reynard," said Mike. "We'll bury Lieutenant Fereaux as decently as we can."

"You know him?" said Delage. "Why, how extraordinary! Could it be that he expected you here and came too soon? But why should he be clothed as a native, if he is a lieutenant of the French Army? Really, I—"

"Really," said Mike, "you talk too damned much!"

Lois sat in her tent, trying not to hear. But the scrape, scrape, scrape of shovels across the field were like fingernails on a blackboard to her.

And then it was quiet and she heard a voice, Mike's voice, drift softly across the open.

"Goodbye, Fereaux."

Chapter Six

THE wind moaned through the passes between the peaks, and all about them stood the Atlas, great black masses, drawn close in darkness, weighing down upon the small camp.

Mike Malloy sat on the machine-gun tripod and shivered as the cold wind stabbed. He did not smoke. At a hundred yards, Berbers thought it no trick, even with bad guns, to knock out a cigarette and, incidentally, the face behind it. He could feel eyes somewhere in the crags, and more than once he started and gripped the machine gun's cocking handle. Such nights, he told himself, were endless. He hated them for the way they sapped a man's nerve and froze the very soul within him.

When morning came he would lose no time in finishing his business and getting out. Quite evidently the bringing of a party into the Atlas had not provided the mask for which General LeRoi had hoped. The Karaouine fanatics had understood at once, and radios had crackled through the Moroccan blue to advance the word. The attack that afternoon had proved one thing very definitely. Something was about to happen here in the Atlas—something which France and Sidi Mohammed, the sultan, must not know. Without doubt, there was a leak in Fez.

The mountains this night would be alive with information

that two espionage agents were on the watch deep in "enemy" territory. And Berbers were careless of life when an idea drove them on. What would it matter if a dozen mountain men died, so long as two French officers were stopped?

Something was happening in the Atlas—something which a pilot could see from a plane, if he searched far enough. That was quite evident. Very well, thought Mike, he would see whatever it was, when there was enough light to see. He would keep up some pretense to the girl and Delage, and would soar out to ostensibly search for the tomb. If possible, he would uncover whatever was happening and then streak for Fez. . . .

Suddenly he was confronted with the other half of the problem. More than he had suspected before, Lois DuGanne was beginning to mean a great deal to him. During the day's excitement she had not shown the white feather, and even when a bullet had come within a foot of her head, showering her with glass, she had not said a word. And he had later seen the burn where the hot empty shell had struck her.

To be sure, she didn't have a very high opinion of him. And suddenly Mike Malloy wanted her to have such an opinion. He wanted her to think he was pretty hot stuff, after all.

That was a new sensation to him. He had always been attractive enough before this. But now a lovely and infinitely desirable woman did not think he measured up very well. How shocked she had been when he had tried to retail the effect of his dark nemesis upon his life. She didn't believe him. She even thought he had been in the wrong during that air fight. But then, she failed to realize that he had been fighting without benefit of a gunner, a fact which far outweighed the greater speed of the French observation plane.

And here she was, staking everything on a silly book which probably didn't exist. . . .

But maybe it did exist. Whether the formula worked or not did not happen to be pertinent to the situation. A thousand-year-old parchment volume about anything would be worth hundreds of thousands, and this one, the only volume missing from the Karaouine Library, would be worth a fortune.

And if he ran away the instant he uncovered Allal Fassei's operations in the Atlas, he would be ruining the girl's chances.

High command never meant much to Mike Malloy. Of course he would carry through with his bargain, and he would get the information if he lived to do it but, at the same time, he had to make certain that he wasn't wrecking Lois DuGanne's life.

It was a sorry mental mix-up for Mike Malloy. And he thought so hard about it that when Reynard came to relieve him, the lieutenant was within ten feet before Mike noticed him.

"Quiet?" said Reynard.

"Too damned quiet," said Mike. "I've got the feeling that they know we're here."

"So have I," said Reynard.

"First thing in the morning I'll take a flight and look things over from the air. If I see anything, I'll radio you, and if I fail to get free, you can take off for Fez in a hurry."

"Right," said Reynard, sitting down on the tripod.

Mike wandered back to his blankets. He sat down and

started to unlace his artillery boots, but he did not finish. He sat silently for several minutes, an uneasy premonition stealing over him. He tied his boots and unloosened the flap of his holster.

Something was warning him not to stay in his bunk. Cold as it was, he gave over the warmth of his blankets. He moved silently up to the edge of the field and sat down beside a broken stone wall, well knowing that it would not be imprudent to have two sentries instead of one. Of course he would pay for his lost sleep in the morning. But it was better to lose sleep than to go to sleep forever.

The dreary hours slowly passed. Mike judged it must be getting close to dawn. He was hungry and he was cold, and his eyelids were leaden.

Abruptly the machine gun clattered madly.

Even before Mike was on his feet, it had stopped. He leaped toward the post.

"It's Mike, Reynard! Where are they?"

It was too dark to see what hit him. The body caromed from his broad chest and started away. Mike made a grab and caught a swirling robe.

He jumped for his quarry and aimed a blow on guess. It connected and his victim grunted, dropping away. Mike was on top of him, trying to hold him down, the djellaba making it difficult to get a good hold on his man. Nails like claws scored down Mike's cheek. He drew back to attack anew.

But the robe was suddenly empty in his hands.

He heard footsteps racing away. An automatic spat near the planes and then there came a shrill, frightened yelp, followed by a yowl of pain. Swift blows smacked, and then the field was again still.

Running toward the ships, Mike shouted, "It's Malloy! Don't shoot!"

A pocket torch clicked on and played its cold beam along the side of the plane. Because the light was not directed at him, Mike could see who held it. Lois DuGanne!

He was instantly at her side, striking the torch down. He caught it and turned it off, and threw her, with himself, upon the earth.

"You want to get killed?" he said sharply.

"You tried hard enough," she panted, spitting out a mouthful of sand.

Mike was up again, running toward the plane. He snapped the torch on and off once, to locate the body he had seen. It was Delage, coming groggily to his hands and knees. Beyond him, Henri was peering with owlish eyes from beneath his blankets.

"I tried to stop him," panted Delage. "He was in the plane."

"Are you hurt?" said Mike.

"Scratched up," said Delage. "I think I nicked him with that shot. There's blood on my shirt."

Mike flicked the light on and off again. He stood listening for some time, but the only sound was the moan of wind through the ravines.

Mike was satisfied that the attacker was gone. He boosted himself into the ship and, cautiously shading the light, found that ruthless hands had ripped the guts out of the radio.

He leaped out and sprinted to the other plane. Again the

light showed him that that set was beyond repair, a hopeless snarl of broken wires frosted with splinters from shattered tubes.

He started back to the ship when he missed Reynard. The lieutenant had made no sound since the first burst of the machine gun.

Mike approached with foreboding.

The first cold gray of dawn was seeping into the eastern sky. It would soon be light.

But not for Reynard.

He lay sprawled across the gun, hands frozen to the trips. Cold grease had jammed a shell, and it was that which had kept the entire belt from running out.

The top of the gun, in that chill light, appeared to be polished. But the polish was moist and warm.

The attacker had hacked Reynard's head half from his shoulders. It had been suddenly done. There was still a stamp of surprise upon the delicately handsome face.

Very gently, Mike carried Reynard to the wall and laid him down, crossing his hands upon his chest. The eyes of the finger ring glittered palely in the half-light.

Delage was there with a shovel. He began to dig.

Mike went to the tents for a blanket and started to pull one from his own rumpled bed. He had thrown his musette bags down upon it when he had left it. And now the blanket would not come free.

He knelt, because it was still very dark in the tent. His questing fingers located the cause—and recoiled from the iciness of steel.

Methodically, with some difficulty, he worked the blade out of the musette bags and blankets, wondering a little at the awfulness of the force which had driven it home in the place where his chest might have been.

It was of Moorish manufacture, that knife. And it was sharp enough to split hairs.

Shaken more than he cared to show, Mike went back to the shallow grave. He rolled Reynard into the cover and helped Delage push back the dirt.

When it was done, Mike stood against the dawn at the head of the unmarked grave.

"Goodbye, Reynard," he said quietly.

Chapter Seven

IT was a dismal breakfast. Henri was obviously frightened out of his wits, and when he thought no one was looking, he would waggle his loosely connected head over his plate with great sadness, as though he were reading in the greasy tin terrible tidings of his own destiny.

Delage was very quiet. His eyes were gray and muddy, and he would stop whatever he was doing to sit tensely, listening, as though his ears were keener than most and could hear things miles and miles away. Ominous things.

All around them stood the craggy peaks of the Atlas, with cover enough to hide a thousand fighting men, and no reason to believe that they did not.

Lois DuGanne's hand shook a little as she poured Mike's coffee. He looked up from his seat on the machine-gun tripod and smiled at her. He knew her kind now. She could keep her chin up through anything, and could carry on as long as necessary. After that she would collapse from nervous exhaustion. But that point was far away. She did not betray her feelings by endless staring at the mountains about them, or by begging for reassurance.

"Good girl," said Mike appreciatively.

"Why? It was my idea that got us into this and I would be a pretty poor sort if I leaned on you now."

Strange words they were, to come from such a fragile and beautiful face.

Mike got up. "Stay by the gun," he said to Henri.

The shadowless man gave a start. He glanced up at the heights. "N-N-No! N-No! I-I wouldn't know what to do. I c-c-c-can't shoot a machine gun."

"You mean you know that the man at the gun is the first target in attack," said Mike, in disgust. "Can you fire one, Delage?"

"I?" said Delage, in amazement. "My dear captain, my mechanical ability is limited to a fountain pen."

"You guys are a lot of help," said Mike. "I've got to shift the gas cargo into my plane and destroy Reynard's. That is, unless either of you gentlemen can fly."

Both Delage and Henri shook their heads vigorously.

Mike turned to the machine gun. "In case somebody knocks me off, this won't be turned on French troops, anyway." He pulled out the loading handle and stuck it in his belt.

Impressing the two men into labor, Mike succeeded in placing the plane at the far side of the field. For a few minutes he worked on the engine and then stepped back, smiling sardonically.

"God help the Berber that fools with that now," he said.

"Why?" said Lois.

"Because I shorted the ignition through the gas lines, and the five gallons of gas I've left in the tank would blow him to glory the second he touched the switch."

He began to empty the salvaged gas into the tank of his

own ship. Lois watched him for several minutes and then, with a shudder, walked slowly back to the camp.

"And now," said Mike at last, "who is going with me? It doesn't much matter, because none of you know machine guns."

"You mean you're going to scout for the tomb?" said Lois eagerly.

"Yes, if you want to put it that way," replied Mike.

"Tell me," said Delage, "aren't you supposed to make some manner of radio report to Fez?"

"Yes."

"Well, then," said Delage, "when they fail to get it this morning, they may suspect that something has happened and send out a squadron to locate us. And if that is the case, someone should make very certain that we can be seen from the air."

Mike looked at him for several seconds. "*M'sieu* Delage, it should by this time be very apparent that all is not well."

"Yes, but—"

"In the first place, the lack of a report will occasion no comment in Fez. They expect it if we are alive. If they don't get it, then—so far as the staff knows—we are dead. No squadron will come for us, Delage. You may as well know it now."

"But I fail to see—"

"No squadron will come, because the act of dispatching a fighting fleet into the Atlas would be likely to blow off the lid. You should have known that Morocco is just waiting for a fuse to be lighted. The explosive is all set. The question is, where and how will it go off? Two planes, under the flimsy guise of an expedition, can enter these mountains. To escape is something else. Unfortunately for you, *M'sieu* Delage, you have come on a suicide mission, and I'm none too hopeful about getting back. You are the pawn—"

"I'll protest to the Minister of War!" cried Delage. "They cannot do this thing to me! I am a man of influence! A word from me—"

"And the French Army does as it pleases," finished Mike.

"I do not believe it," said Delage.

"I do not believe it," echoed Henri.

"Your belief is not necessary to the truth," said Mike. "Now consider. Those two who stay here can remake the camp on that cliff face so as to command the field with rifles, in case of attack. The one who goes with me goes into probable aerial combat. Allal Fassei seems to have planes in the Atlas—though God knows from whence they came."

Henri looked at the sky and turned a little green. Delage looked at the face of the cliff and began to pick up baggage for the shifting of the camp.

Mike looked at Lois. "They have unanimously elected you, like the gallant Frenchmen that they are. If I did not need an observer, you could stay here. But I happen to need one and, further, there is a chance that you can locate your *L'Aud*. That is, if you have any idea—"

"Oh, I have!" cried Lois. "The place was charted within a mile. My uncle worked it out from a Moor chart of the Atlas which he discovered in an old book. It was buried with Ibn Tumart."

"Then let's go. Looking for one thing, I expect to find another."

"You'll be back for us?" begged Henri.

"Though it will probably be difficult," said Mike, "yes." He smiled a little. "The French Army may not care about you, but you two would be heavy on my conscience."

"I didn't know you had one," said Lois.

Without comment, he helped her into the ship and then slid into his own seat, sliding the hood into place. He started the engine and warmed it carefully.

Taxiing into the wind, he saw that both Henri and Delage were watching him forlornly. He waved to them, but they were too despondent to wave back. He clipped the throttle and the ship surged forward, blasting the echoes of the Atlas and laying a screen of dust across the valley.

The peaks slipped below them, and Mike glanced back to see if Lois was taking it well. It startled him a little to find that she was examining a small chart which she had taken from her pocket.

"What a woman!" he said admiringly to himself.

Chapter Eight

TO the south, in a hidden reach of the Atlas, lay a field which had been painstakingly cleared and leveled to make a runway a quarter of a kilometer long. Along this narrow stretch many great sheets of canvas had been stretched on poles and painted to simulate earth. A score of planes were so masked, and with widespread wings they seemed to crouch in the shelters, waiting for the cry of war.

Bombers they were, and their bomb bays were full of cylindrical death. Within two hours these great, fast ships could lay the French fields and barracks of Fez in ruins.

Mechanics worked on motors, the sleeves of their djellabas rolled back and their skirts greasy. Pilots, not yet needed, lounged in canvas shade, smoking innumerable cigarettes and bragging what would be done when the command was given. Their training had been long, and their service longer. Deserters from a dozen armies were here, Fassei gold jingling in their pockets and hopes of high position making them gloat over the future's prospects.

The far-off drumming of a motor struck silence across the field. Men swiftly sought cover. A masked battery of antiaircraft machine guns was manned, and hungry muzzles waited to bay at the sky.

But the plane which began to slide on sighing wings down the sky was without insignia, and men again moved into the open.

The ship, a fast two-seater of German design, taxied to a dusty landing. The man in the gunner's pit stood up, and a sweeping shout blasted across the field. "Allal Fassei!" Pilots, gunners and mechanics crowded about.

Allal Fassei was a fit fellow to lead such a crew. His djellaba was crimson, and a damascene dagger balanced the automatic at his belt. The face was withdrawn into the hood, but the features were not masked. They were sharp and Arabic, and the eyes were hot as any zealot's. Allal Fassei bared his black teeth in a grin.

"I salute you, my brave ones," he said as he raised his hand, palm outward. "I come to tell you that all is in readiness."

"When?" they cried.

"Three days," said Allal. "And then the foreign dogs shall look into the air and meet death. And when they try to run, they will find in every beggar and shopkeeper an armed and fighting soldier. The sultan will bar himself in his palace, to discover death at the hands of his own guard. Even now, the arms are being distributed, the word is being passed. In three days, no infidel Christian in Morocco shall be alive!"

They cheered him until the best of them were hoarse. The echoes rolled like cannon fire through the gorge.

Allal permitted them to lift him down. Some of them were excited about the plane in which he rode. It was the very latest in aircraft, armed with .50-caliber machine guns.

A Berber chief named Zaig, who had once been the athletic pride of Oxford, stepped forward. He was in command of the drome.

"Master," said Zaig, "there has been news received from Fez. In these mountains this very minute, army espionage is at work. Under the blind of a quest for the book, *L'Aud*—"

Allal laughed sharply. "You think I would remain ignorant of this for long? Every shrub in Morocco has ears listening for Allal Fassei. I paused with the Rualla, and I have even further news. Last night commendable enterprise saw to it that Lieutenant Reynard was killed. The Rualla say that he unhappily fired a warning before he died, thus making it impossible for the others to be killed, since there was no way of knowing whether or not another machine gun covered the camp. A certain infamous captain named Malloy, and three dupes of some political importance, are still alive. It is probable that Malloy will scout for this field. Perhaps he knows what is here, perhaps he does not. But if France knew, then no such pair of officers would have been dispatched. Their radios are wrecked and they cannot communicate with Fez.

"Three of you take the air and try to find this Captain Malloy. Some others will go to the field and trap him, should he fail to be found in the air. We have done for the other agents throughout the Atlas. He is the last, and we must take no chances on his escaping."

Zaig turned and told off three pilots, who immediately moved toward a squadron of ready pursuit planes.

51

It was all a minor detail to Allal Fassei. He walked excitedly beside Zaig.

"To think," said Allal, "that all Morocco will be in our hands within three days!"

"It has been long in coming," said Zaig prayerfully. "But Allah is good!"

Chapter Nine

MIKE was there to look over the ground and discover, if he could, any possible troop concentrations. Consequently it was of little moment exactly where he went, and he followed the girl's directions, all the while watching on his own.

She had been looking anxiously for half an hour, trying to discover a peak which was split like a gunsight, and now she found it. Snowcapped against the blue, there was no mistaking it.

Excitedly she shook Mike's shoulder. "There it is!"

He located it, still greatly preoccupied with his ground search.

"What is its compass bearing?" she asked.

He took it as three hundred and six degrees.

"It should be approached at three hundred and fifty," she said. "And then, twenty-seven kilometers away from its base, we will find two intersecting ravines, above which there is a small plateau. You'll try, won't you?" she pleaded.

He caught some of her excitement. It would do no great harm to at least locate the site, and so, continuing his ground search, he corrected the approach.

He was puzzled at the emptiness of the villages, the lack of rifle fire from the ground. For all he could see, the last Berber in the Atlas had vanished.

He was still preoccupied with his problem when she again smote his shoulder.

"There are the ravines!" she cried.

He looked down and saw them, somewhat amazed at the accuracy of her information. "How do you know this will lead you to *L'Aud*?" he asked.

"A man spent thirty years tracing this," said Lois. "I would be witless indeed if I couldn't follow directions."

"You ought to have been a surveyor."

"Did you think I left on such a search without studying something?"

"If you'd studied gunnery, it would have been more to the point," said Mike.

"There's the plateau!" she cried. "And now, down that other hill there should be the ruins of an old Roman caravanserai. Ibn Tumart's sultanate was on that hill to the right, and his tomb was on the bank of a creek . . . There's the creek!"

He put one wing down and slowly turned on it, looking at the tumbled walls of the ancient buildings. There were many such in the Atlas—too many for comment, built by races both remembered and forgotten, and leveled by wars which had even vanished from history. And so, despite his Atlas service, he had never before noticed this particular cluster of broken building stone.

"Can we land?" she pleaded.

He looked at her and then at the earth, which appeared to be turning below them. The plateau had a two-thousand-foot diameter. It was strewn with boulders, large and small. But if wind permitted and piloting skill could be fully employed, there was a chance.

"Okay," said Mike, "we're going down. But don't feel bad if we never take off again."

He cut the gun and leveled out. He banked, and the rough ground sped up to them at an alarming rate.

Here the wind was treacherous with crosscurrents caused by the roughness of the terrain, and gust after gust tossed the two-seater about.

Face tense, Mike fought the controls. A wing skimmed a giant boulder. A wheel struck and bounced. A blast of air sent the ship careening toward a pyramid of rock. Mike shot the gun on for an instant and straightened out.

The wheels touched and the plane was jarred by a series of impacts. Finally the dust settled and the motor ran out, and they were safe in the quiet of the Atlas sunlight.

Mike mopped his brow and looked at Lois. He realized that she had not appreciated the danger of that landing, or else she was too overcome with reaching the end of her search.

She was out of the plane in a moment, running toward the ramp which led down to the ravine from the plateau. She stopped and looked back.

"Aren't you coming?" she called.

He got out and scanned the sky. The uneasy knowledge that the French plane had probably been spotted made him hesitate. But Lois was already halfway down the broken ramp, which had once been trod by the feet of Roman legions. He followed.

For the ensuing two hours they combed the ruins, Lois ever in front, eyes bright with excitement, all danger forgotten, face smudged with the ancient dust.

At last she pointed ahead. "There! I told you it was here! Mike, look!"

He saw a conical structure, like a beehive grown to bungalow dimensions. The thing was carved by centuries of wind, and it looked very worthless and forlorn.

"That's it!" shouted Lois, running toward it.

Mike came up and sat down on a stone slab. Lois walked all around it, looking for an entrance and discovering none. At last she returned helplessly to Mike.

"Isn't there some way we can get in?" she pleaded.

Calmly he reached into his shirt and brought out a bundle of dynamite, to which a cap was already attached. She missed this fine disregard for safe practice.

"I was saving it for Berbers," said Mike, "but it's all in a good cause."

He drilled a hole the height of his head and inserted the dynamite. He lighted the fuse and raced back. The explosion was loud, and the soft, eroded stone crumpled under the downward burst.

Mike took a pocket torch and stepped in.

Ibn Tumart was there, beyond doubt. At least all that was mortal of the famous man—a few grains of dust in a metal box. Berbers had a superstition about tombs, but Lois was not hampered.

She began by sounding the box and, finding nothing,

examined the pedestal on which it stood. A fine cloud of dust rose.

Mike, meanwhile, inspected the walls. And it was Mike that found *L'Aud*.

Not being able to appreciate the thirty years of preparation and research which had gone into its discovery, and having only to reach into a niche and bring forth a silver box, well preserved in this dry climate, he did not consider that the book could be worth much.

He looked at it lying in its small coffin and was struck by curiosity about the gold formula. Lois, with a glad cry, came to his side. Hastily she took it from him. "Don't touch it! It's liable to fall apart!"

She used a small knife to lift the pages, and soon confirmed the volume's identity. "Here it is! 'Antimony boiled with zinc in the black of the moon, to which must be added a pinch of hair from a two-year-and-seven-months-old gazelle . . .'"

"That won't work," said Mike practically. "It takes electronic bombardment of—"

"Of course it won't. But that doesn't detract from the fact that this is an archaeological treasure. Why, men have been looking for this book for centuries. . . ."

"Well, there it is," said Mike, glad because she was glad. "Now how about getting upstairs, before somebody spots our ship and gets ready for a reception."

Chapter Ten

CLUTCHING the silver box, Lois sat back in her seat. She was too elated and overcome with success to pay much attention to anything else, and Mike had to buckle her chute straps on her shoulders. She scarcely knew what he was doing.

Mike started the engine and examined the poor excuse for a runway ahead. He had to go in that direction, if he wanted to use the wind. Five hundred feet in front, the plateau ended in a gorge. He had to take a chance on the help of an updraft, because he would drop over the lip without sufficient flying speed and run the chance of crashing into the cliff beyond the chasm.

He started. He held his breath as he fought his way through the stones. The ground blurred and then was gone. Below, a stream sparkled and the plane started to sink toward it. A gust of air caught the wings and sent them hurtling skyward. The opposite cliff was grazed by the wheels, which spun madly as Mike fought to get far aloft.

At last he was clear, and building altitude. He grew conscious of the moisture on his brow and hands. With a look of relief he turned to Lois.

But she had scarcely seen what had happened. At first it made him somewhat angry to have his two skillful flying victories so lightly regarded.

"You might at least say, 'Gosh'" reproved Mike. "It isn't human not to be scared stiff when you go through something like that."

She looked at him in wonder, realizing that he was actually a little put out at her. "But," she said without thinking, "you're at the controls and I know you'll see us through no matter what—" She stopped suddenly, realizing what confidence she had expressed, as though frightened that he would misunderstand.

He grinned at her. "I'm a louse, but you trust me," he coaxed.

"Why shouldn't I trust you? I'm sure that your character hasn't much to do with your fighting skill."

It brought him down for a moment. But he had no time to ruminate on her swift check.

High above them three planes were flying in tight formation. They were pursuit ships, and their absence of all insignia was insignia enough.

"I hope you're right," said Mike, pulling back and beginning a fast climb for advantageous altitude. "We've got callers."

The sight of those three hovering planes drove all triumph out of her. Her hands clutched *L'Aud*'s silver case and she winced under the threat of losing that for which she had sought so long. Anxiously she looked at Mike's wide shoulders.

He wasn't as natty now as he had been. The khaki was stained with dust and grease, and his shoulders were dark with sweat. But in the hood glass she could see his strong profile and the glint of determination which had come into his bright Irish eyes.

The two-seater was boring sky, and the earth was all crazy and aslant below, and the three ships above were waiting with calm circles, as though more than certain of their prey.

Mike drilled straight at them, as though extremely anxious to meet them. And they saw and confidently let him come.

At twelve thousand feet, with another two thousand to go, Mike changed tactics. Abruptly he leveled out and put his nose down and ran for it.

For seconds the pursuit ships did not realize what he was doing, and when they did, they had lost most of their advantage. They swooped as one into a dive which would bring them close to the French ship's tail.

Mike let his throttle full out and the ship shivered under the drive of speed.

"Are you trying to get back to the field?" said Lois.

"If we can lose these guys, we'll get Delage and Corvault. If we can't lose them, and are still ahead, we're going to Fez. I think I know what's happening in the Atlas. Those ships are the best made in any totalitarian country."

At long range, the others opened fire. Occasionally their tracer came close enough for their smoke to be shredded by the French plane's slipstream.

It soon became apparent that Mike did not have any edge of speed. Slowly the trio was coming closer, and more frequently chattered their guns.

Suddenly the fabric which bore the insignia of France ripped loose and fluttered madly behind the right wingtip, a blur of red, white and blue.

Mike dived to pick up more speed. Full out and heading straight, they were fast approaching the landing field where they had left Delage and Henri.

But the pursuit planes also dived, and a blast of lead tore out a strut from the two-seater's left wing. It banged for a moment, tearing a great hole in the lower foil's fabric, and then went tumbling into the distance.

"Hold on!" said Mike.

Suddenly he yanked back on his stick. The loop was so swift that the centrifugal force almost crushed Lois. The world went black as the blood left her head.

She was stung to life by the scorching smell of cordite and the battering concussion of the bow guns.

Straight ahead, a pursuit ship was streaking to get away. The pilot glanced back, and then he was something scarlet in a helmet. The plane yawed and started straight up. Lois saw it whipstall and begin its spin and then a new sound made her face quickly front.

The French engine had developed a loud, grinding noise. The prop splintered into fragments. A pursuit ship lanced overhead and banked to come around.

Mike kicked the switch shut and pushed his stick into the panel. The two-seater started straight down, and all the Atlas leaped skyward toward them, jagged and yellow.

Lois felt as though her head were about to split in two pieces. Nothing could stand such a dive, entered at three hundred miles an hour and now risen to five hundred.

Mike didn't intend anything to stand it. "You'll have to

jump. The rip cord is over your heart. Feel to see if your heart is still beating, and count three and pull."

She started to push at the hood. But the earth straight ahead was an awful thing.

"I can't!" she cried. "Oh, God, I can't!"

Mike looked at her. At five hundred miles an hour straight down he found an instant to grin. "You're human after all," he shouted, pulling slowly on the stick.

The two-seater's dive became slowly shallow and the speed grew less. But any attempt to get all the way out of that dive with the injured wings would have undressed the plane.

Mike threw back the hood and the air roared past like ten hurricanes. He grabbed *L'Aud* and shoved it under his chute harness. He grabbed Lois' arm and the pain of his strong hand stung her into action. Suddenly she was hurtling with him through space. She could see the world, all mixed with Mike and clouds and pursuit planes high above.

But they were slowing down, and the world was still a thousand feet below. The two-seater had long gone.

"Pull your rip cord when I yell!" said Mike.

She could not stand the falling, she tried to grab at the ring.

"Do you want to get killed?" he bellowed at her.

And in an instant, *"Pull!"*

He released her and she jerked the ring. She could not see him and terror gripped her. She felt the shrouds running out, and then with a jolt which seemed hard enough to break her apart, the chute opened.

Directly under her was a field, and the wind bore her half

down its length in a brace of seconds. She was whirling so that she still could not see Mike. She expected bullets, and was half puzzled that they did not come.

Suddenly her feet dragged on a downward swing and, despite the fact that she landed tense, she was not hurt. Very strangely, hands had kept her from crashing into the ground and men were spilling the wind from her chute.

In alarm, she stared about her and gradually the dizziness of the whirling fall left her.

The men who were responsible for her easy landing were cloaked in djellabas, rifles slung across their backs. They grinned familiarly at her.

Then she saw Mike. Very calmly he spilled his own chute and stood on it while he disengaged his harness. Men were running toward him, carrying rifles in both hands.

Among them was a fellow in a scarlet robe, and it was to him that Mike called out in Arabic.

"Greetings, Allal Fassei," said Mike, carefully pulling the silver box from under his arm. "Thank me for saving you from your own ignorance."

Allal Fassei motioned and men eased their firing pins down.

"It was very funny," said Mike, "to have to fight so hard to keep your men from destroying this very rare object."

Allal Fassei approached swiftly. "What have you there, spy?"

"Spy?" said Mike. "A spy in full uniform? Not guilty, Allal. True, I was looking around for you, but with tricolor flying. This, my venerable creator of riot, will probably interest you. It is nothing less than the one missing book from the

Karaouine, *L'Aud,* containing the mystic and magic formula for the making of gold."

Allal snatched for it like a jackal grabbing fresh meat.

The men, enlivened by the magic word, "gold," came as close to Allal as they dared.

"Restore that to the Karaouine and you gain even more prestige," said Mike. "It would show your extreme sympathy with the priests."

Allal Fassei stared at the unconcerned officer. "You give me this? Though you know it places all question of success from my uprising? You give me such prestige, when you could have thrown it away?"

"Naturally," said Mike. "You are noted for your knowledge of government affairs, Allal. That is the one thing which the government does know about you. Perhaps you recall that a certain officer named Captain Malloy trounced three staff officers in a moment of madness and was then sentenced to prison and the *bataillon pénal.* I am Captain Malloy."

"Ah," said Allal, beginning to think he understood.

"And my perseverance at locating *L'Aud* to ensure success to your revolt should give you some indication of my loyalty. I have been waiting for this chance. I regret the necessity of shooting down a plane while we still had radio communication and this battle just now—which I had to fight to save *L'Aud.* My unquestionable talents as a fighting officer are completely at your command."

Allal looked at him for a long time. He was still not convinced. "Perhaps I can use you when the attack starts.

It depends, of course, on behavior, and as I am a man of prudence, I shall keep you under guard. Tonight I shall radio Fez to check on you—someone may know something there, you see. In the meantime, you have earned your life."

"By the way," said Mike, "don't touch that French plane over there. It's wired to blow up, and even I would not like to chance that because of the risk. Keep away from it."

"Abd Deg," called Allal, "put the captain under guard, pending further information."

"What might have happened to two men I left here?" said Mike.

"Shot," shrugged Allal.

"One was important in France," replied Mike.

"No one will know until it is too late," said Allal with a shrug.

"And the young lady," said Mike, "is an American. A man about to set up a new government should be cautious about neutrals."

"When I need your advice, Captain, I shall ask for it. Abd Deg, also place the woman under guard. We are leaving for the drome."

The men fell into line with their Moorish barbs.

Lois was close to the breaking point. Her courage had been carried by hope, but now she had seen *L'Aud* carelessly handed to a cutthroat rebel. She made no resistance as they placed her on a horse. She hardly realized that Mike was riding beside her, until he spoke.

"Don't worry," he said. "Things could be worse."

She looked at him bitterly. "I understood most of what you said."

He lifted his brows, with a shrug of fatalism. "The fortunes of war can best be swung by a man with an ability for lying."

"Maybe you weren't lying," said Lois wearily.

"The lady," Mike told the sky, "certainly does have a horrible opinion of Mike Malloy!"

Chapter Eleven

THE afternoon sun was hot in the camouflaged drome, but the men of Allal Fassei were too intent upon the prospects of slaughter and loot to be dulled by mere solar heat. They paraded through the canvas hangars, boasting to one another and occasionally picking a quarrel about future spoils.

The sentry who had been posted before the stone hut to guard the prisoners was not at all satisfied with his lot. But as long as Allal Fassei was in camp, he had to look very alert.

The hut itself was fairly cool, and for that the philosophic Mike Malloy was very grateful. He was thankful for other things. These men were too intent upon future spoils of war to worry very much about immediate quarry. Had they been bored, the fate of Lois DuGanne would have been a certain, sealed affair. As it was, they paid scant attention to the presence of a woman in camp, except to spit as they passed the hut door, to show their contempt for infidels. It happened that many of them were renegades Christian-born. But religion is an easy thing to a mercenary.

Lois was too disheartened to mind the sordid surroundings. Ordinarily she would have disdained such a bed, which might have other, smaller occupants. But now she had flung herself face downward upon it, face buried in her arms.

Mike walked up and down the room, thankful also that this was the only strong building in the place and, therefore, their mutual jail.

"Don't take it so hard," said Mike. "You never can tell what will happen."

Her voice was muffled. "You're safe enough. I . . . I believe you'd fight for Allal if you had to."

"Maybe," said Mike. "It's certain the French never thought much of my inestimable value."

"I believe you would lie yourself out of anything!"

"It's an art," said Mike. "Look, dear lady, don't take all this so hard. If Allal finds out I'm all right for his purposes, all we have to do is pretend that you belong to me and there won't be any argument—"

"Belong to you?" cried Lois, looking up. "A self-confessed murderer and embezzler and deserter and—"

"Don't try to think up any more," said Mike. "That's plenty. I told you none of it was my fault. My luck just runs this way. The man I shot in Cochin China was going to shoot me in a duel, wasn't he? And I tried to . . . Aw—aw, what's the use. Everything I've ever done has turned out backwards. I wanted you to like me, and I've even made a mess of that."

She looked quickly at him.

"Yes, that's right," said Mike. "I wanted you to think I was a swell guy, so I didn't lose any time trying to show you that everything that was said about me wasn't entirely true. Law has a habit of looking at the cold facts, and not what lies behind them. As a matter of fact, the only thing which was ever hung on me was busting three staff officers because—"

He stopped and went to the window.

"Why did you fight them?"

"Aw, you wouldn't be interested," said Mike.

"I might be."

"Well, a sergeant was flogging a spahi, and I took the whip away from the sergeant to show him how it felt and these staff officers saw it, and told me that I wasn't a spahi and had no authority over the punishment and that, in the second place, I was interfering with discipline. I wouldn't give the whip up, so the aide tried to take it away from me and . . . well, I picked him up and threw him at the colonel and the lieutenant colonel, and . . ."

"So that's how you landed in jail," said Lois.

He was glad to see that he had diverted her attention from her immediate woes. "Sure. You don't do things like that on African service. Everybody is always jumpy, and especially at a time like this, with our friend Allal trying to blow the place apart."

"What will you do if he accepts you for service?"

"I don't know," said Mike. "He'll find out two things from his Fez agents. He'll discover why I went to jail, and then he'll also find out that, no matter what else I've done, I've never sold anybody out. If he finds out the latter—" He drew his forefinger across his throat and Lois shuddered. "That," he added, "is the price of having a reputation for loyalty. But maybe he won't find it out. There's one thing certain. If I don't get information to Fez about this lovely layout here, *le Maroc* as a French possession is finished."

"Do you think Allal will succeed?"

"How can he help it? He's got these dopey natives believing that the French are responsible for drought and windstorms and the size of the sun. They think they'll be happy under Allal. And Allal is just a puppet for the dictators. The woes of *le Maroc* will have just begun. But they can't see it. France has been too easy on them. And because she has been easy, about fifty thousand troops will be eased to *Shaitan*'s tender mercies, and not ten white men will be alive in the whole country. God, if we'd only known that he was bringing these bombers in from the south! But it seems so impossible that he would be able to get them. I can't understand it. Allal Fassei is just a two-bit marionette, so far as anybody knows—but then nobody knows."

He drifted to the door and looked through the ironwork at the sentry. "Going to be lots of fun around here pretty soon," he said.

"I can't talk to you," growled the Berber.

Mike drifted back and sat down on the table. It was very wobbly on its legs and with sudden interest he inspected it.

Soon he lost interest and, having talked himself out, stared thoughtfully at the wall.

Lois watched him.

Slowly time wore away and the long shadows began to merge with the dusk.

Mike approached the sentry. "Isn't it time we had some food?"

"No orders to give you food."

"But we can't starve," said Mike. "That would be—" He broke off, seeing a tall Berber approach.

Zaig paused with one boot on the step and looked through the ironwork at Mike. "We have received word from Fez," said Zaig in broad English, "and we regret exceedingly, old chap, that our agent there thinks you a most interesting liar. He heard, you see, your conversation with General LeRoi. It is then my unpleasant duty to take you out and shoot you. All you fellows are the same."

"No such word as mercy in your vocabulary, is there," commented Mike.

"Mercy? Where a French officer is concerned? You amuse me. Unlock the door, sentry."

Keys rattled, and then Mike did an unexpected thing. He turned to Lois and pulled her toward him. "Please," he said to Zaig, as the Berber stepped in, "tell me what is to become of this woman?"

"Perhaps I have a use for her," smiled Zaig. "I early learned to appreciate white women."

Fiercely, Mike held Lois close to him. He startled her by almost kissing her. But he turned angrily to Zaig. "You might have enough courtesy to look away!"

Zaig grinned and turned around.

The table came down and the leg crushed Zaig's skull almost in the same instant. Mike swung the club a second time, straight into the sentry's face. He caught the rifle before it fell and swiftly snaked the body inside.

"There's one white woman you'll never appreciate," said Mike, as he dropped the dead Berber into the corner.

He started toward the door and stopped. On the field, the fleet German two-seater had been wheeled into line. Allal

Fassei, bound for another concentration point and depending on coming moonlight by which to land, was climbing into his cockpit.

His pilot received his signal and took off. As the plane flashed by, Allal was just pulling on his helmet.

Mike drew back. "They'll find us out in a moment. We haven't a chance to steal a plane. Somehow we'll have to run for it. Are you game?"

She clutched his hand and followed him through the door.

They swiftly went through the gathering darkness, their way masked by the hut, until they had climbed a considerable distance up the side of a hill. After that, it was easier going and more difficult to be seen.

Before they were out of sight of the camp, Mike looked back.

"Some soldiers," he said. "Empty gas drums lined up in the first hangar."

"Let's go," shivered Lois.

He turned and they sped through the gloom.

Chapter Twelve

LOIS had lost all sense of direction and forgotten that one can steer by the stars. Accordingly she was astounded, two hours later, to find that they were scrambling down a steep slope into the field on which they had first landed.

"Praise Allah," said Mike. "They took my word about the plane."

He went swiftly to work upon it and, with little trouble, reconnected the gas lines and ignition in their proper places. He went back among the rocks and turned up the spare gas supply, which he had drained out of the ship, and with Lois' help made short work of filling the tank.

As he helped her into the pit, he looked into her face for a moment. She caught her breath, but he only eased her into the seat and handed her the ends of the belt to be buckled.

He started the engine. The roar, which seemed to blast the very stars, made Lois fear they would certainly be heard and apprehended before they got away.

But Mike calmly let the gauges come up to pressure and temperature and then, to Lois' relief, taxied out into the rocky runway and blasted wide open down the stretch.

It was difficult to see the ground, despite the orange glow given off by the rising moon. She hardly knew when earth and ship parted.

Building altitude in steady spirals, Mike brought the moon into sight. It was weirdly beautiful, looking as though it had been washed with blood.

Lois began to wonder if Mike had really lost his way this time. He kept on going up, up, up, without ever heading north toward the safety of Fez.

But she did not question him. She merely wondered about it, and felt safe and weary. This cockpit was much larger than that of the other ship and she could stretch out at length.

She knew she must have slept, because she had no knowledge of when the engine had stopped.

For an instant she thought it was Fez, and then knew there had not been time enough. Again she thought they were landing, but when she looked about the moon-bathed peaks, she saw that they were thousands of feet above them.

In a steady, silent glide, the two-seater was going down the sky. It was creepy to ride a silent plane along the path of the moon with all the world of sharp mountains bathed in red below.

On and on they went, with never a sound except the gentle whisper of the floating wings.

And then she saw their objective.

Few lights were showing, but they were enough. The moonlight completed the picture. What had appeared to be a long strip of cultivated field became, suddenly, the drome of Allal.

And still they made no sound.

"Hold on tight," said Mike, "this is going to blow us all over the sky."

She gripped the cowl, looking straight ahead at the shadowy drome.

And then Mike started the engine. It burst forth with its strident song. The plane quickened pace and the earth shot toward them.

Suddenly a long streamer of green flame raked up at them. An antiaircraft machine gun had started. Instantly there were others, clattering hysterically.

Mike swooped across the field. It seemed inevitable that he would crash into the first hangar. It grew mountainous before them.

The earth was fully light with powder flame, and the din was ear-shattering.

Mike pressed his machine-gun trips. The burst was deep into the hangar, probing for the empty gasoline drums, as explosive as bombs under the fire of tracer bullets.

Nothing happened, and he pulled up so steeply that he almost ran his wheels on the canvas edge.

The loop would have been death, if it had not been so perfect. The two-seater came out of it and streaked straight back at the hangar, guns going like trip-hammers.

And this time, tracers hit.

With a flash of flame, a drum exploded. Mike was going straight up and the concussion had not yet hit the ship.

The first drum took a second, and then a dozen went together. And all down the long row of bombers, bomb bays were jammed with high explosive, set to detonate at the slightest jar.

Straight up went the two-seater. The first wave of concussion hit it and sent it like a leaf in a hurricane—but upward, toward the zenith.

Then the explosions came all together in one vast roar. It seemed that the very Atlas were splitting asunder. The heavens were alight and the gleaming cliffs were spattered with soaring debris.

Mike fought the ship level before it could spin. He was shaken a little, and he looked back at Lois. She was white of face, but she nodded that she was all right.

He started to streak north toward Fez, but a shadow flicked across the two-seater.

Mike turned and looked up, to behold, silhouetted against the moon, the fast two-seater which had carried Allal Fassei away that afternoon.

Allal Fassei, returning, had seen the havoc, and now he saw the cause—and seeing was madness. In a superior ship, with a machine gun in his hands, he yelled his pilot down to destruction.

The world was still alight with the burning field. Allal could see the insignia and know. And with bullets streaking like balls of flame from the rear-pit guns, Allal swung into battle.

Without a gunner of his own, there was only one thing which Mike could do. He verticaled tightly and stabbed straight at the oncoming plane.

A thousand yards became a hundred in the flash of an instant. But Mike did not break. Thumbs hard down on his machine-gun trips, he made a javelin of his plane.

It was a threat which could not be withstood. It was the other man who broke. He yanked wildly back on his stick.

A fraction of a second later, so did Mike.

Wheels to wheels, the two planes hurtled toward the stars. But Mike was below the other. Allal could not use his guns in that position. Mike could.

Throwing his lances of lead just ahead of the other ship, Mike succeeded in accomplishing his purpose. He went over on his back in a sloppy stall, his flying speed gone. The other whipstalled and headed for the earth.

Without engine, there was only one thing which Allal's ship could do, and that was land on the still-burning field. Bombs had taken the guns and men. Bombs had taken the planes which had intended to drop them on Fez.

Allal's pilot leveled out and volplaned. Mike followed at a watchful distance while Allal, in one last burst of frenzy, strove to bracket the French ship. But the shots were wide.

The engineless plane leveled out. But the air was hot and bumpy. Only a miracle man could have put a ship on that runway without an engine. Allal's pilot was not a miracle man.

At the first touch of the landing gear, Allal's pilot struck a hole gouged out by bomb fragments. The ship somersaulted and crashed upon its back.

Sailing smoothly in, and waltzing like a dancer around the shell holes with stick and engine, Mike put the French ship down.

He looked watchfully around the field. But there was no menace here now. He examined Allal's plane from afar, but the man who would never be the dictator of *le Maroc* was hanging by his knees from his belt, without a thought of fight.

Mike secured his gun and cut him down. Allal sprawled on the smoking earth, looking dazedly at the chaos which reigned. Mike cut the pilot out of his cockpit and boosted him over to Allal.

"You're an important man in France," said Mike. "Can't afford to lose you now. The War Department would be extremely wroth to have anything happen to you."

Allal Fassei scowled darkly.

"And if we wash some of that stain off your face, along with the pencil lines," said Mike, "I am pretty certain that we would find *M'sieu* Delage and timid little Henri Corvault, who thought machine guns were horrible. Come, gentlemen, the firing squad of France awaits you."

"How did you know?" said Delage in a croaking voice.

Mike plucked *L'Aud* from under the djellaba. It was uninjured. "You wanted to gain face with the people by giving this to the Karaouine. That sealed your prestige. You didn't become interested or answer Miss DuGanne until your revolt looked certain. And again, Delage, only you could have tried to murder me and then slaughtered Reynard. Berbers, I might remind you, do not like to fight in the dark, and would never have the courage to enter such a camp alone. They would have come by the hundreds. And your knife, *M'sieu* Delage, bore the legend, 'Made in Hamburg.' Just a moment, until I tie you up, and we'll be going."

Chapter Thirteen

THE dress parade was colorful and the Legion band was in very fine form.

General LeRoi came down the parade ground to where the Air Service stood.

He stopped. "*Capitaine* Michael Ste. Marie Jacques Malloi Du Vincennes!"

Mike stepped a stiff pace forward, looking very grave.

"For conspicuous gallantry beyond the limits of duty," said General LeRoi. He pinned the medal on Mike's chest and then brushed Mike's cheeks with his white mustache, and the parade was over.

The Legion went, playing quick time, and the troops broke formation and various officers, among them a colonel, a lieutenant colonel and an aide, shook Mike by the hand and told him they always knew he was a fine fellow.

And Mike passed the general, as he searched through the crowd for a certain person, and heard the general say, "No, I have never made an error. It is my excellent judgment of men which has made . . ."

The press was taking it down.

Suddenly a long staff car drew up and a captain yelled at Mike. "I've got your baggage. You'll miss the train!"

Mike, looking anxiously around, approached the car. He lifted his bright red, blue and gold cap and scratched his head.

"Gosh, I'd of thought she'd stay for that!" said Mike, bewildered. He got into the car and stood up, still looking for Lois.

"Love?" said the captain.

"Naw," said Mike. "Finance."

Suddenly Lois was before him, brightly smiling, eyes very proud of him. He leaned over, and though she looked up at him, he made no offering.

"Look," he said. "The French government is going to give you five hundred thousand francs as your share of *L'Aud*. They are presenting it to the Karaouine and they'll get plenty of face by doing it." He was anxious. "Is that all right with you?"

"Oh, yes. You . . . you're going away, Mike?"

"Me? Oh, sure. The family found out what a fine fellow I was in the newspapers. . . . Here," he fished a radio message out of his hat. "'Certain you would enjoy Paris. Have appointment as air advisor waiting. We await you with gladness. All my love, General Malloi Du Vincennes.'"

"But I thought . . . I thought maybe you . . . might celebrate your medal. . . ."

The French captain kicked Mike sharply on the boot. It was disastrous. Mike almost fell out of the car. Lois saved him.

"Are you going to Paris?" said Mike suddenly.

"Why, yes . . . yes! I'm going to Paris."

"Well, what the hell are we waiting for?" said Mike. "Get in!"

Story Preview

Story Preview

NOW that you've just ventured through one of the captivating tales in the Stories from the Golden Age collection by L. Ron Hubbard, turn the page and enjoy a preview of *Arctic Wings*. Join Constable Bob "Lawbook" Dixon, the toughest manhunter in Canada's Royal Mounties. Dixon's known for keeping to the very letter of the law while bringing harsh justice to the Arctic, but events turn swiftly against him when he's framed for murder and becomes fair game for those out to settle old scores.

Arctic Wings

THEY came into the post with little ceremony. The older one said, "This Taggart, Streak?"

"Yeah," said Streak.

"Taggart, I'm Bob Dixon. Heard of me?"

Evidently Taggart had, as Nancy noticed him flinch. She looked with new respect at Constable Pilot Bob Dixon. Yes, there was steel in the man, and his face was as emotionless as though carved from iron. His gaze was level and penetrating. He had not glanced toward Nancy.

"We thought you'd be here," said Dixon. "Would you like to tell what you know about the Hanlon killing or shall I knock it out of you?"

"It's a lie," said Taggart, bristling and stalking forward. "It's a lie. I didn't have nothin' to do with Hanlon's shooting."

"I didn't say he was shot. And it happened night before last up at his placer." Dixon smiled without a hint of humor. "Keep on talking, Taggart. You'll hang sooner or later and this might as well be the time."

"Hang, will I?" said Taggart. "To hell with you, Mountie. I said I didn't know. . . ."

Suddenly Bob Dixon's big fist balled up and crashed into Taggart's jaw. Taggart went down to his knees, shaking his head. Dixon yanked him to his feet and struck again but this time Taggart rushed. Dixon ducked and threw his weight sideways and sent the bigger man hurtling against the wall.

Deliberately, the Mountie advanced, jerked the man to his feet, plucked out the Colt and slammed Taggart down into a chair. Dixon did not appear to be ruffled. There was no anger in him, only thoroughness.

"Maybe he didn't do it," said Streak Faulkner, staring at Taggart's bloodied face.

"All rats are the same," snapped Dixon. "Even if he didn't, he's given more beatings than he's taken."

"Yeah," said Streak in a melancholy way, "but I think you go too far with this stuff sometimes, Bob."

Suddenly Nancy knew the Mountie. She had heard of him time after time. They called him "Lawbook" Dixon, but she had not known that he had been ordered to the Tokush River country.

Dixon slapped Taggart away with his gauntlets. Taggart lunged to get out of the chair but a hard blow smashed him back.

Nancy felt a little sick. She went out of the porch and looked at the lake but the day was no longer so crystal bright. In the room she heard an occasional blow and once a chair went over. And in a blood-chilling monotone, Dixon kept asking over and over about the killing. Taggart's voice was getting weak and once Streak interposed. He was a good kid, Streak. A little reckless and without too many brains, but men liked him.

At last they dragged Taggart out on the porch. The bully was a bully no more. His face was swollen and thick and his beard was dyed red in spots. Terror had its grip on him. His bedeviler had not even showed signs of weariness.

"If you didn't do it," said Dixon, relentlessly, "then how is it you have so many pound notes? Hanlon had a cache, they tell me, and it's empty. There were pound notes in that cache."

"I didn't get them from Hanlon!" cried Taggart, beaten down.

"Then where did they come from?" said Dixon.

"I'll tell you," whimpered Taggart. But he didn't. He sagged between them as though he was going to pass out.

Nancy watched because she couldn't look away. Taggart was tough and this was the first time Taggart had ever been whipped, that was plain. But he had been whipped and this chunk of granite in khaki, this Mountie without a heart, had done it without half trying. She did not recognize the cunning of intelligent training there.

They started to let Taggart down to the puncheon boards but he had only been shamming. With a wild back sweep of his arms, he sent both Mounties reeling and leaped off the porch to sprint for his canoe.

Dixon got up on one knee. "Stop, in the King's name!"

Taggart was too frightened to stop. He made the gunwale. The explosion of powder was like a physical blow to Nancy. She saw Taggart stiffen, half in and half out of the craft. Gradually he sank sideways into the water and streamers of red fanned out from him.

89

Dixon walked down to him and pulled him to the shore. Taggart's hip was shattered by the big Webley slug and he slowly came around, moaning in pain.

"Damn you," whispered Taggart, "I was straight for once. Straight! The Crees been selling furs and I've been selling them bullets and traps and they had pound notes. I didn't know nothing about the Hanlon killing."

Streak patched him up with a first-aid kit and the two Mounties loaded him into the police ship.

"Take him down to Fort Ledeau," said Dixon. "I'll wait here."

"Okay," said Streak. "But I kinda wish you hadn't shot, Bob."

"All rats are the same," said Dixon.

Streak turned and taxied out into the lake and headed into the wind. He took off with a steep, climbing turn to give vent to his feelings.

Bob Dixon walked slowly back to the porch. "Sorry, Miss . . ."

"Nancy McClane."

He took off his helmet. "They're all the same, those fellows. They're yellow at heart and they terrorize every weaker person they meet. Say, that must have been nasty, having that fellow drunk on your hands. I'm glad we happened in."

"I was in no danger," said Nancy. "You are not the only one that knows tricks."

He looked at her admiringly. "One wouldn't connect wrestling tricks with such a pretty girl—if you'll pardon me, Miss McClane. Say, you talk like a Yank."

"Yes."

"That's swell," said Dixon, but gravely. "My mother was a Yank. Are you up here with your father?"

"My father is dead."

"Oh. I'm sorry. Was he from this country?"

"From Virginia," said Nancy.

That struck a chord in Dixon. He frowned a little, searching his police file brain and then, eyes wide open in astonishment, he looked at Nancy and his calm was gone.

"Why . . . why that must have been Thomas McClane who was—" He stopped, embarrassed and now more than a little uneasy.

"Go ahead," said Nancy, coolly. "I see now why they call you 'Lawbook' Dixon. Go ahead. Certainly I'm the daughter of a criminal and criminals are all rats. Certainly. They arrested Thomas McClane for selling fraudulent stocks on a loaded mine and they put him in prison and he got tuberculosis and died. He was a gentleman, not a rat."

Uncomfortable, on more than one count, Dixon turned and went down to sit on the edge of the wharf and watch for Streak's return.

To find out more about *Arctic Wings* and how you can
obtain your copy, go to www.goldenagestories.com.

Glossary

Glossary

STORIES FROM THE GOLDEN AGE *reflect the words and expressions used in the 1930s and 1940s, adding unique flavor and authenticity to the tales. While a character's speech may often reflect regional origins, it also can convey attitudes common in the day. So that readers can better grasp such cultural and historical terms, uncommon words or expressions of the era, the following glossary has been provided.*

---

antimony: a brittle, lustrous white metallic element, used chiefly in alloys.

Atlas: Atlas Mountains; a mountain range in northwest Africa extending about fifteen hundred miles through Morocco, Algeria and Tunisia, including the Rock of Gibraltar. The Atlas ranges separate the Mediterranean and Atlantic coastlines from the Sahara Desert.

barbs: a breed of horses introduced by the Moors (Muslim people of mixed Berber and Arab descent) that resemble Arabian horses and are known for their speed and endurance.

bataillon pénal: (French) penal battalion; military unit consisting of convicted persons for whom military service was either assigned punishment or a voluntary replacement of imprisonment. Penal battalion service was very dangerous: the official view was that they were highly expendable and were to be used to reduce losses in regular units. Convicts were released from their term of service early if they suffered a combat injury (the crime was considered to be "washed out with blood") or performed a heroic deed.

Bedouin: a nomadic Arab of the desert regions of Arabia and North Africa.

Berbers: members of a people living in North Africa, primarily Muslim, living in settled or nomadic tribes between the Sahara and Mediterranean Sea and between Egypt and the Atlantic Ocean.

boon: something to be thankful for; blessing; benefit.

bracket: to place (shots) both beyond and short of a target.

caravanserai: a roadside inn where travelers could rest and recover from the day's journey. Caravanserais supported the flow of commerce, information and people across the network of trade routes covering Asia, North Africa and southeastern Europe. Typically it was a building with a square or rectangular walled exterior, and a single doorway wide enough to permit large or heavily laden beasts, such as camels, to enter. The courtyard was almost always open to the sky, and the inside walls of the enclosure were outfitted with a number of identical stalls, bays and niches or chambers to accommodate merchants and their servants, animals and merchandise.

Cochin China: a region covering southern Vietnam. Originally part of the Chinese empire, it was made a French colony in 1867 and combined with other French territories to form French Indochina in 1887 with Saigon as its capital. It was incorporated into Vietnam in 1949.

Colt: revolver manufactured by the Colt Firearms Company, founded in 1847 by Samuel Colt (1814–1862), who revolutionized the firearms industry with the invention of the revolver.

cordite: a family of smokeless propellants, developed and produced in the United Kingdom from the late nineteenth century to replace gunpowder as a military propellant for large weapons, such as tank guns, artillery and naval guns. Cordite is now obsolete and no longer produced.

cowl: a removable metal covering for an engine, especially an aircraft engine.

Crees: North American Indians living in central Canada.

damascene: metal, such as iron or steel, decorated with wavy patterns of etching or inlays of precious metals, especially gold or silver.

Dieu: (French) God.

djellaba: a loose-hooded cloak of a kind traditionally worn by Arabs.

drome: short for airdrome; a military air base.

emplacement: a prepared position for weapons or military equipment.

Fez: the former capital of several dynasties and one of the holiest places in Morocco; it has kept its religious primacy through the ages.

foil: airfoil; any surface (such as a wing, propeller blade or rudder) designed to aid in lifting, directing or controlling an aircraft by using the current of air it moves through.

Four Hundred, the: the wealthiest and most exclusive social set of a community.

glass jaw: a jaw that is excessively fragile or susceptible to punches.

G-men: government men; agents of the Federal Bureau of Investigation.

gunwale: the upper edge of the side of a boat. Originally a gunwale was a platform where guns were mounted, and was designed to accommodate the additional stresses imposed by the artillery being used.

Hadith: one who follows the way of life prescribed for Muslims on the basis of the teachings and practices of Muhammad and interpretations of the Koran.

Ibn Tumart: (1080–1130) Berber religious teacher and founder of the ruling dynasty of the twelfth century in the region that is now Morocco. He founded a monastery in the Atlas Mountains that served as an important religious center. It is also his burial site.

ice-wagon: a slow-moving vehicle.

Irish Guard: Irish Legion of the French Army, created by Napoleon in 1803 with the intention of invading the British Isles. Irish nationalists saw the Irish Legion as a means of liberating Ireland from British rule and so many enlisted. When the planned invasion did not take place, some of the Irishmen quit though the greater majority remained and fought for Napoleon with distinction. At his coronation in 1804, Napoleon presented the Irish Legion with an eagle (bronze eagle sculpture mounted on top of the blue regimental flagpole), the only one he ever entrusted to a foreign corps, along with their own flag. In 1813, after seeing firsthand the fighting valor of the Irish Legion in battle, he granted them the honor of guarding him.

Karaouine University Library: university in Fez, Morocco, founded in 859 and one of the oldest universities in the world. It is associated with the city's giant mosque and is considered one of the most important centers of learning in North Africa.

kepi: a cap with a circular top and a nearly horizontal visor; a French military cap that men in the Foreign Legion wear.

Lebels: French rifles that were adopted as standard infantry weapons in 1887 and remained in official service until after World War II.

Légions Étrangères: (French) Foreign Legion; a specialized military unit of the French Army, consisting of volunteers of all nationalities assigned to military operations and duties outside France.

le Maroc: (French) Morocco.

Lewis gun: a gas-operated machine gun designed by US Army Colonel Isaac Newton Lewis in 1911. The gun weighed twenty-eight pounds, only about half as much as a typical medium machine gun. The lightness of the gun made it popular as an aircraft-mounted weapon, especially since the cooling effect of the high-speed air over the gun meant that the gun's cooling mechanisms could be removed, making the weapon even lighter.

M. or *M'sieu:* (French) *Monsieur;* Mr.

ma foi: (French) my faith; an exclamation used to emphasize an accompanying remark or to express surprise, etc.

Middle Atlas: part of the Atlas Mountain range lying in Morocco. It is the westernmost of three Atlas Mountain chains that define a large plateaued basin extending eastward into Algeria.

M'm'selle: (French) *Mademoiselle;* Miss.

Monte Carlo: a town of Monaco on the Mediterranean Sea and the French Riviera. It is a noted resort famed for its casinos and luxurious hotels.

Moorish barbs: a breed of horses introduced by the Moors (Muslim people of mixed Berber and Arab descent) that resemble Arabian horses and are known for their speed and endurance.

Morocco: a country of northwest Africa on the Mediterranean Sea and the Atlantic Ocean. The French established a protectorate over most of the region in 1912, and in 1956 Morocco achieved independence as a kingdom.

musette: a small canvas or leather bag with a shoulder strap, as one used by soldiers or travelers.

placer: a waterborne deposit of gravel or sand containing heavy ore minerals, as gold, which have been eroded from their original bedrock and concentrated as small particles that can be washed out.

puncheon: large timbers with one flattened side, usually used for flooring.

Riff: a member of any of several Berber peoples inhabiting the Er Rif, a hilly region along the coast of northern Morocco. The Berber people of the area remained fiercely independent until they were subdued by French and Spanish forces (1925–1926).

Rualla: the name of an Arab tribe.

sacré nom d'un cochon: (French) damned name of a pig.

Saigon: city in southern Vietnam and capital of French Indochina (now Ho Chi Minh).

Scheherazade: the female narrator of *The Arabian Nights*, who during one thousand and one adventurous nights saved her life by entertaining her husband, the king, with stories.

Shaitan: (Arabic) Satan.

shock troops: assault troops; infantry formations and their supporting units intended to lead an attack.

shrouds: the ropes connecting the harness and canopy of a parachute.

slipstream: the airstream pushed back by a revolving aircraft propeller.

Sorbonne: a university in Paris; intellectual center of France.

spahi: a member of a light cavalry regiment of the French Army recruited primarily from Algeria, Tunisia and Morocco.

stall: a situation in which an aircraft suddenly dives because the airflow is obstructed and lift is lost. The loss of airflow can be caused by insufficient airspeed or by an excessive angle of an airfoil (part of an aircraft's surface that provides lift or control) when the aircraft is climbing.

strut: a support for a structure such as an aircraft wing, roof or bridge.

Toutou: (French) doggie; used as an endearment.

tracer: a bullet or shell whose course is made visible by a trail of flames or smoke, used to assist in aiming.

tricolor: the French national flag, consisting of three equal vertical bands of blue, white and red.

volplaned: glided toward the earth in an airplane, with no motor power or with the power shut off.

whipstall: a maneuver in a small aircraft in which it goes into a vertical climb, pauses briefly, and then drops toward the earth, nose first.

white feather: a single white feather is a symbol of cowardice. It comes from cockfighting, and the belief that a gamecock sporting a white feather in its tail is not a purebred and is likely to be a poor fighter.

Yank: Yankee; term used to refer to Americans in general.

L. Ron Hubbard
in the Golden Age
of Pulp Fiction

*In writing an adventure story
a writer has to know that he is adventuring
for a lot of people who cannot.
The writer has to take them here and there
about the globe and show them
excitement and love and realism.
As long as that writer is living the part of an
adventurer when he is hammering
the keys, he is succeeding with his story.*

*Adventuring is a state of mind.
If you adventure through life, you have a
good chance to be a success on paper.*

*Adventure doesn't mean globe-trotting,
exactly, and it doesn't mean great deeds.
Adventuring is like art.
You have to live it to make it real.*

— *L. RON HUBBARD*

L. Ron Hubbard
and American
Pulp Fiction

B ORN March 13, 1911, L. Ron Hubbard lived a life at least as expansive as the stories with which he enthralled a hundred million readers through a fifty-year career.

Originally hailing from Tilden, Nebraska, he spent his formative years in a classically rugged Montana, replete with the cowpunchers, lawmen and desperadoes who would later people his Wild West adventures. And lest anyone imagine those adventures were drawn from vicarious experience, he was not only breaking broncs at a tender age, he was also among the few whites ever admitted into Blackfoot society as a bona fide blood brother. While if only to round out an otherwise rough and tumble youth, his mother was that rarity of her time—a thoroughly educated woman—who introduced her son to the classics of Occidental literature even before his seventh birthday.

But as any dedicated L. Ron Hubbard reader will attest, his world extended far beyond Montana. In point of fact, and as the son of a United States naval officer, by the age of eighteen he had traveled over a quarter of a million miles. Included therein were three Pacific crossings to a then still mysterious Asia, where he ran with the likes of Her British Majesty's agent-in-place

L. Ron Hubbard, left, at Congressional Airport, Washington, DC, 1931, with members of George Washington University flying club.

for North China, and the last in the line of Royal Magicians from the court of Kublai Khan. For the record, L. Ron Hubbard was also among the first Westerners to gain admittance to forbidden Tibetan monasteries below Manchuria, and his photographs of China's Great Wall long graced American geography texts.

Upon his return to the United States and a hasty completion of his interrupted high school education, the young Ron Hubbard entered George Washington University. There, as fans of his aerial adventures may have heard, he earned his wings as a pioneering barnstormer at the dawn of American aviation. He also earned a place in free-flight record books for the longest sustained flight above Chicago. Moreover, as a roving reporter for *Sportsman Pilot* (featuring his first professionally penned articles), he further helped inspire a generation of pilots who would take America to world airpower.

Immediately beyond his sophomore year, Ron embarked on the first of his famed ethnological expeditions, initially to then untrammeled Caribbean shores (descriptions of which would later fill a whole series of West Indies mystery-thrillers). That the Puerto Rican interior would also figure into the future of Ron Hubbard stories was likewise no accident. For in addition to cultural studies of the island, a 1932–33

LRH expedition is rightly remembered as conducting the first complete mineralogical survey of a Puerto Rico under United States jurisdiction.

There was many another adventure along this vein: As a lifetime member of the famed Explorers Club, L. Ron Hubbard charted North Pacific waters with the first shipboard radio direction finder, and so pioneered a long-range navigation system universally employed until the late twentieth century. While not to put too fine an edge on it, he also held a rare Master Mariner's license to pilot any vessel, of any tonnage in any ocean.

Yet lest we stray too far afield, there is an LRH note at this juncture in his saga, and it reads in part:

"I started out writing for the pulps, writing the best I knew, writing for every mag on the stands, slanting as well as I could."

To which one might add: His earliest submissions date from the summer of 1934, and included tales drawn from true-to-life Asian adventures, with characters roughly modeled on British/American intelligence operatives he had known in Shanghai. His early Westerns were similarly peppered with details drawn from personal experience. Although therein lay a first hard lesson from the often cruel world of the pulps. His first Westerns were soundly rejected as lacking the authenticity of a Max Brand yarn

Capt. L. Ron Hubbard in Ketchikan, Alaska, 1940, on his Alaskan Radio Experimental Expedition, the first of three voyages conducted under the Explorers Club flag.

(a particularly frustrating comment given L. Ron Hubbard's Westerns came straight from his Montana homeland, while Max Brand was a mediocre New York poet named Frederick Schiller Faust, who turned out implausible six-shooter tales from the terrace of an Italian villa).

Nevertheless, and needless to say, L. Ron Hubbard persevered and soon earned a reputation as among the most publishable names in pulp fiction, with a ninety percent placement rate of first-draft manuscripts. He was also among the most prolific, averaging between seventy and a hundred thousand words a month. Hence the rumors that L. Ron Hubbard had redesigned a typewriter for faster keyboard action and pounded out manuscripts on a continuous roll of butcher paper to save the precious seconds it took to insert a single sheet of paper into manual typewriters of the day.

That all L. Ron Hubbard stories did not run beneath said byline is yet another aspect of pulp fiction lore. That is, as publishers periodically rejected manuscripts from top-drawer authors if only to avoid paying top dollar, L. Ron Hubbard and company just as frequently replied with submissions under various pseudonyms. In Ron's case, the list

A MAN OF MANY NAMES

Between 1934 and 1950, L. Ron Hubbard authored more than fifteen million words of fiction in more than two hundred classic publications. To supply his fans and editors with stories across an array of genres and pulp titles, he adopted fifteen pseudonyms in addition to his already renowned L. Ron Hubbard byline.

Winchester Remington Colt
Lt. Jonathan Daly
Capt. Charles Gordon
Capt. L. Ron Hubbard
Bernard Hubbel
Michael Keith
Rene Lafayette
Legionnaire 148
Legionnaire 14830
Ken Martin
Scott Morgan
Lt. Scott Morgan
Kurt von Rachen
Barry Randolph
Capt. Humbert Reynolds

included: Rene Lafayette, Captain Charles Gordon, Lt. Scott Morgan and the notorious Kurt von Rachen—supposedly on the lam for a murder rap, while hammering out two-fisted prose in Argentina. The point: While L. Ron Hubbard as Ken Martin spun stories of Southeast Asian intrigue, LRH as Barry Randolph authored tales of

L. Ron Hubbard, circa 1930, at the outset of a literary career that would finally span half a century.

romance on the Western range—which, stretching between a dozen genres is how he came to stand among the two hundred elite authors providing close to a million tales through the glory days of American Pulp Fiction.

In evidence of exactly that, by 1936 L. Ron Hubbard was literally leading pulp fiction's elite as president of New York's American Fiction Guild. Members included a veritable pulp hall of fame: Lester "Doc Savage" Dent, Walter "The Shadow" Gibson, and the legendary Dashiell Hammett—to cite but a few.

Also in evidence of just where L. Ron Hubbard stood within his first two years on the American pulp circuit: By the spring of 1937, he was ensconced in Hollywood, adopting a Caribbean thriller for Columbia Pictures, remembered today as *The Secret of Treasure Island.* Comprising fifteen thirty-minute episodes, the L. Ron Hubbard screenplay led to the most profitable matinée serial in Hollywood history. In accord with Hollywood culture, he was thereafter continually called

The 1937 Secret of Treasure Island, *a fifteen-episode serial adapted for the screen by L. Ron Hubbard from his novel,* Murder at Pirate Castle.

upon to rewrite/doctor scripts—most famously for long-time friend and fellow adventurer Clark Gable.

In the interim—and herein lies another distinctive chapter of the L. Ron Hubbard story—he continually worked to open Pulp Kingdom gates to up-and-coming authors. Or, for that matter, anyone who wished to write. It was a fairly unconventional stance, as markets were already thin and competition razor sharp. But the fact remains, it was an L. Ron Hubbard hallmark that he vehemently lobbied on behalf of young authors—regularly supplying instructional articles to trade journals, guest-lecturing to short story classes at George Washington University and Harvard, and even founding his own creative writing competition. It was established in 1940, dubbed the Golden Pen, and guaranteed winners both New York representation and publication in *Argosy*.

But it was John W. Campbell Jr.'s *Astounding Science Fiction* that finally proved the most memorable LRH vehicle. While every fan of L. Ron Hubbard's galactic epics undoubtedly knows the story, it nonetheless bears repeating: By late 1938, the pulp publishing magnate of Street & Smith was determined to revamp *Astounding Science Fiction* for broader readership. In particular, senior editorial director F. Orlin Tremaine called for stories with a stronger *human element*. When acting editor John W. Campbell balked, preferring his spaceship-driven tales,

Tremaine enlisted Hubbard. Hubbard, in turn, replied with the genre's first truly *character-driven* works, wherein heroes are pitted not against bug-eyed monsters but the mystery and majesty of deep space itself—and thus was launched the Golden Age of Science Fiction.

The names alone are enough to quicken the pulse of any science fiction aficionado, including LRH friend and protégé, Robert Heinlein, Isaac Asimov, A. E. van Vogt and Ray Bradbury. Moreover, when coupled with LRH stories of fantasy, we further come to what's rightly been described as the foundation of every modern tale of horror: L. Ron Hubbard's immortal *Fear*. It was rightly proclaimed by Stephen King as one of the very few works to genuinely warrant that overworked term "classic"—as in: *"This is a classic tale of creeping, surreal menace and horror. . . . This is one of the really, really good ones."*

L. Ron Hubbard, 1948, among fellow science fiction luminaries at the World Science Fiction Convention in Toronto.

To accommodate the greater body of L. Ron Hubbard fantasies, Street & Smith inaugurated *Unknown*—a classic pulp if there ever was one, and wherein readers were soon thrilling to the likes of *Typewriter in the Sky* and *Slaves of Sleep* of which Frederik Pohl would declare: *"There are bits and pieces from Ron's work that became part of the language in ways that very few other writers managed."*

And, indeed, at J. W. Campbell Jr.'s insistence, Ron was regularly drawing on themes from the Arabian Nights and so introducing readers to a world of genies, jinn, Aladdin and Sinbad—all of which, of course, continue to float through cultural mythology to this day.

At least as influential in terms of post-apocalypse stories was L. Ron Hubbard's 1940 *Final Blackout*. Generally acclaimed as the finest anti-war novel of the decade and among the ten best works of the genre ever authored—here, too, was a tale that would live on in ways few other writers imagined. Hence, the later Robert Heinlein verdict: "Final Blackout *is as perfect a piece of science fiction as has ever been written.*"

Like many another who both lived and wrote American pulp adventure, the war proved a tragic end to Ron's sojourn in the pulps. He served with distinction in four theaters and was highly decorated for commanding corvettes in the North Pacific. He was also grievously wounded in combat, lost many a close friend and colleague and thus resolved to say farewell to pulp fiction and devote himself to what it had supported these many years—namely, his serious research.

Portland, Oregon, 1943; L. Ron Hubbard captain of the US Navy subchaser PC 815.

But in no way was the LRH literary saga at an end, for as he wrote some thirty years later, in 1980:

"Recently there came a period when I had little to do. This was novel in a life so crammed with busy years, and I decided to amuse myself by writing a novel that was pure science fiction."

114

That work was *Battlefield Earth: A Saga of the Year 3000*. It was an immediate *New York Times* bestseller and, in fact, the first international science fiction blockbuster in decades. It was not, however, L. Ron Hubbard's magnum opus, as that distinction is generally reserved for his next and final work: The 1.2 million word *Mission Earth*.

> **Final Blackout**
> *is as perfect*
> *a piece of*
> *science fiction as*
> *has ever*
> *been written.*
>
> —Robert Heinlein

How he managed those 1.2 million words in just over twelve months is yet another piece of the L. Ron Hubbard legend. But the fact remains, he did indeed author a ten-volume *dekalogy* that lives in publishing history for the fact that each and every volume of the series was also a *New York Times* bestseller.

Moreover, as subsequent generations discovered L. Ron Hubbard through republished works and novelizations of his screenplays, the mere fact of his name on a cover signaled an international bestseller. . . . Until, to date, sales of his works exceed hundreds of millions, and he otherwise remains among the most enduring and widely read authors in literary history. Although as a final word on the tales of L. Ron Hubbard, perhaps it's enough to simply reiterate what editors told readers in the glory days of American Pulp Fiction:

He writes the way he does, brothers, because he's been there, seen it and done it!

THE STORIES FROM THE GOLDEN AGE

Your ticket to adventure starts here with the Stories from
the Golden Age collection by master storyteller L. Ron Hubbard.
These gripping tales are set in a kaleidoscope of exotic locales and brim
with fascinating characters, including some of the
most vile villains, dangerous dames and brazen heroes
you'll ever get to meet.

The entire collection of over one hundred and fifty stories is being
released in a series of eighty books and audiobooks.
For an up-to-date listing of available titles,
go to www.goldenagestories.com.

AIR ADVENTURE

117

FAR-FLUNG ADVENTURE

SEA ADVENTURE

TALES FROM THE ORIENT

The Devil—With Wings
The Falcon Killer
Five Mex for a Million
Golden Hell
The Green God
Hurricane's Roar
Inky Odds
Orders Is Orders

Pearl Pirate
The Red Dragon
Spy Killer
Tah
The Trail of the Red Diamonds
Wind-Gone-Mad
Yellow Loot

MYSTERY

The Blow Torch Murder
Brass Keys to Murder
Calling Squad Cars!
The Carnival of Death
The Chee-Chalker
Dead Men Kill
The Death Flyer
Flame City

The Grease Spot
Killer Ape
Killer's Law
The Mad Dog Murder
Mouthpiece
Murder Afloat
The Slickers
They Killed Him Dead

119

FANTASY

Borrowed Glory	*If I Were You*
The Crossroads	*The Last Drop*
Danger in the Dark	*The Room*
The Devil's Rescue	*The Tramp*
He Didn't Like Cats	

SCIENCE FICTION

The Automagic Horse	*A Matter of Matter*
Battle of Wizards	*The Obsolete Weapon*
Battling Bolto	*One Was Stubborn*
The Beast	*The Planet Makers*
Beyond All Weapons	*The Professor Was a Thief*
A Can of Vacuum	*The Slaver*
The Conroy Diary	*Space Can*
The Dangerous Dimension	*Strain*
Final Enemy	*Tough Old Man*
The Great Secret	*240,000 Miles Straight Up*
Greed	*When Shadows Fall*
The Invaders	

120

WESTERN

The Baron of Coyote River
Blood on His Spurs
Boss of the Lazy B
Branded Outlaw
Cattle King for a Day
Come and Get It
Death Waits at Sundown
Devil's Manhunt
The Ghost Town Gun-Ghost
Gun Boss of Tumbleweed
Gunman!
Gunman's Tally
The Gunner from Gehenna
Hoss Tamer
Johnny, the Town Tamer
King of the Gunmen
The Magic Quirt

Man for Breakfast
The No-Gun Gunhawk
The No-Gun Man
The Ranch That No One Would Buy
Reign of the Gila Monster
Ride 'Em, Cowboy
Ruin at Rio Piedras
Shadows from Boot Hill
Silent Pards
Six-Gun Caballero
Stacked Bullets
Stranger in Town
Tinhorn's Daughter
The Toughest Ranger
Under the Diehard Brand
Vengeance Is Mine!
When Gilhooly Was in Flower

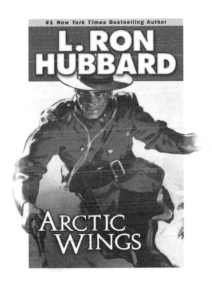